WAYLAND BABES

WAYLAND BABES

JUDI DAYKIN

This edition produced in Great Britain in 2021

by Hobeck Books Limited, Unit 14, Sugnall Business Centre, Sugnall, Stafford, Staffordshire, ST21 6NF

www.hobeck.net

Text: copyright © Judi Daykin 2021

Front cover image: copyright @ Gwynira Daikin 2021

This book is entirely a work of fiction. The names, characters and incidents portrayed in this novel are the work of the author's imagination. Any resemblance to actual persons (living or dead), events or localities is entirely coincidental.

Judi Daykin has asserted her right under the Copyright, Design and Patents Act 1988 to be identified as the author of this work.

All rights reserved. No parts of this book may be used or reproduced by any means, graphic, electronic, or mechanical, including photocopying, recording, taping or by any information storage retrieval system without the written permission of the copyright holder.

A CIP catalogue for this book is available from the British Library.

ISBN 978-1-913-793-50-0

Cover design by Jayne Mapp Design, with front cover image by Gwynira Daikin

Printed and bound in Great Britain by Clays Ltd, Elcograf S.p.A

❀ Created with Vellum

Are you a thriller seeker?

Hobeck Books is an independent publisher of crime, thrillers and suspense fiction and we have one aim – to bring you the books you want to read.

For more details about our books, our authors and our plans, the chance to enter competitions, plus to download *Crime Bites*, a free compilation of novellas and short stories by our authors sign up for our newsletter at www.hobeck.net.

You can also find us on Twitter **@hobeckbooks** or on Facebook **www.facebook.com/hobeckbooks10**.

For Rhett, Gwynira, Ellie and Martin

1649

Now, ponder well, ye parents dear,
These words which I shall write;
A doleful story you shall hear,
In time brought forth to light.
A gentleman of good account
In Norfolk dwelt of late,
Who did in honour far surmount
Most men of his estate.

Sore sick he was, and like to die
No help his life could save;
His wife by him as sick did lie,
And both possest one grave.
No love between these two was lost,
Each was to th' other kind.
In love, they liv'd, in love, they dy'd
And left two babes behind.

Chapter One

It seemed to Henry that the whole world was weeping. The February wind drove drenching sheets of water across the track, soaking him and making his horse, Oliver, shake his head to empty his ears. Henry spread his cloak across the back of the horse in a vain attempt to try and protect them both. Water dripped from the brim of his Roundhead helmet onto his face. It mixed with the snot from his nose. Raising his gloved hand, he wiped at the wet, which was replaced in minutes by more: the glove, the leather of the saddlery and the wool of his cloak stank of damp animal. Horse and human scent melded into one.

They had set out early from their overnight lodgings in Attleborough. The public house had been warm, the stables well kept, the ale acceptable, and the costs no more outrageous than anywhere else on his journey from London. The war had pushed up prices everywhere. If they were lucky, it would be no more than a single day's ride to his home on Green Farm, close to Little Massingham.

They were not lucky. The grey of early morning turned to darker skies. The rain had grown heavier until here they were, soaked through and on a track that should take them in the right direction if only Henry could see it properly. Oliver shook his head in frustration and blew that half-snort, half-whinny that his rider knew meant the poor creature was getting tired.

A battle-hardened warhorse was a prized possession. Henry always put his companion's needs before his own. Reining to a stop, he swung down onto the track, hefted the cloak over the saddle and, loosely holding the reins, began to walk beside the horse.

'A rest for your back,' he said, rubbing under the mane to comfort Oliver. 'Come now, emulate the courage of your namesake, Ironside, and we shall find a village soon. Unless this storm has washed them all away.'

It was hard to tell how long they had been walking. They had left Attleborough as the church clock struck eight, which was a good start given the shortness of the days. The weather had removed any sense of what time of day it was, and Henry struggled to work out how long they had been moving.

He thought that he knew many of the green lanes hereabouts. As a boy, he had often accompanied his father to markets in the area. That was before the war had begun, seven long years ago.

Enraged by the King's arrogance and suspicious of his Catholic wife whispering endless poison in his ear, the Puritans of Parliament had rebelled. Henry did not pretend to understand what had happened. But he believed his preacher, who, week on week, thundered his disapproval of Catholic religious practices and vanities. Henry's father had talked of the Divine Right of Kings. He claimed this gave the King the excuse he wanted to treat his subjects with contempt and tax them out of existence.

'Outrageous,' he would shout. 'Good, hard-working people like us should not be expected to pay extra tax for the King's fine clothes and fancy foreign wars.'

At first, Henry had looked on in envy as other young men joined their respective sides. His father had refused him permission to join, even though he was sixteen and a strong rider.

'No good will come of this,' he said. 'Besides, I need you on the farm.'

News, when it came, seemed to prove his father right. The fighting had been vicious, the outcome of the battles often uncertain, and the parliamentarians suffered heavy casualties.

'We should stay out of it,' he'd said to Henry. 'They won't trouble us all the way out here.'

But he had been wrong. One day, Lord Ireton had descended with armed men and culled half their herd of cows to feed the Royalist army without a penny of compensation. A few weeks later, Henry accompanied his father to hear Oliver Cromwell speak in Ely and instantly joined the Army of Eastern Association.

He had followed his hero from that day, rarely returning to his home. Filled with the passion of religious righteousness, sure of his vocation, emboldened by his continued survival on the battlefield against all likelihood, Henry had worshipped Oliver Cromwell. Until the end of January.

On the last day of that month, he had set out for home. Leading his faithful Oliver stealthily away from the cavalry picket line and passing through the London streets in the early morning dark, he left the army without notice or permission. For they had killed the King, and Henry had watched them do it.

Chapter Two

The soldier and the horse trudged on. The rain was turning to sleet, its icy fingers beating a painful rhythm on Henry's jacket and the sodden cloak that dragged downwards from Oliver's back. Henry could barely see the ground that slipped and slid beneath his feet. Oliver's head hung low, his neck strained to keep his face out of the worst of the weather. It was getting darker. Both of them were soaked to the bone and shaking with cold.

As they walked dejectedly beside each other, Henry wondered whether they should pull into the shelter of the next group of trees. He knew they must be getting close to the barren Brecks by now. There the sheep ate the grass low, and the wind blew what few bushes dared to grow into strange shapes. It was a place where there was little chance of finding a friendly copse. The storm showed no sign of easing. Henry's belief in God, so recently shaken to the core, offered only the comfort that came from habit. Nonetheless, he muttered a fervent plea to God for deliverance and safety, adding a mumbled Lord's Prayer for good measure.

As if in answer, after a few more steps the hedges on either side of the track began to look more tended. Surely, Henry reasoned, they must come to shelter soon. The wind blustered in all directions. Sleet drummed now in their faces, now on their backs. The light was failing, and Henry steered Oliver by the white outlines of the hedgerows or the freezing edges of deep puddles. Surely no one would be out in this storm unless they had to be. So why did his ears, ringing with hours of effort and cold, now find amongst the bluster the sound of whispered laughter? The voices of small children? Henry anxiously strained to listen. Oliver stamped nervously.

'Who's there?' he called. His voice was lost in the storm as soon as it left his mouth. The only reply came from Oliver, pulling on the bridle to step forward. Too weary to wonder, Henry followed his horse.

A few more agonising minutes brought the pair to the outskirts of a hamlet. There were a handful of unkempt cottages, a barn with its roof almost gone, and an alehouse at the top of the road. The small squat building let out a welcome warm light from its narrow windows. Smoke from the chimney promised a fire within. As Henry led Oliver around to the rear, they were relieved to find a small yard with a couple of stables.

'Ho! Aid needed,' Henry called. A door banged open, and a middle-aged woman appeared.

'Lord bless you, sir,' she bellowed. 'You'll be needing shelter indeed. Saul. Saul!'

A giant of a man lumbered up behind her. Pushing him bodily out into the yard, she pointed to Oliver.

'Do you help the poor creature,' she instructed. 'The end stable is free, and make sure you rub him down well. Come with me, sir. My son, Saul, will see to your horse.'

Saul took the reins from Henry, patted Oliver on the neck, then clicked expertly to the weary horse, who followed him willingly enough. The woman gestured for Henry to follow her inside.

The taproom was tiny, its ceiling low. Red pamment tiles covered the floor, a table glowed with lanterns, and another door led deeper into the house. The fire was stacked up and blazing, a pile of logs waiting to hand. A pair of settles guarded the hearth. Two older, weather-beaten men occupied them, one on either side. They watched him with open curiosity as one pulled up his legs to slide along the bench so that Henry could get close to the warmth.

'Don't you mind those two, sir,' the woman said, taking his jacket and hanging it on the end of the settle to dry. 'My name's Mary. I'm mistress of this establishment. Now, you get warm. Take off your boots if you want to. I'll mull you some of my elderberry wine.'

Mary set a poker in the embers, then bustled out through the far door. The man opposite Henry nodded to him.

'I'm George,' he said. 'You'll like that. It be her speciality. You come far?'

'From Attleborough.'

'Only that far? Shame.' He sounded disappointed. 'Thought you might have some news, you being in uniform and all.'

'News?'

'Of the war.'

'The war is over.'

There was a silence as the man looked at his neighbour, then studied his beer. Finally, he asked, 'Did we win?'

'In a manner of speaking, yes.'

Henry struggled to pull his soaking boots from his feet. They had been good leather once, but had been so often repaired that they were now almost falling to pieces. He had only managed to remove one when Mary returned with a tankard.

'Couldn't you help the man, George?' she demanded, waving at the two men to move out of her way. With more strength than Henry would have suspected, she tugged the other wet boot from his leg and placed the pair close enough to the hearth to warm without getting scorched. Then pulling the poker from the fire, she wiped it quickly with a cloth and plunged it into the tankard, setting the contents to bubble and steam.

The outside door slammed as Mary handed the brew to Henry. Saul had returned, a sack over his shoulders to ward off the rain, Henry's sodden cloak in his arms. Dropping the sack to the floor, he hung the cloak over the drying rack, which he raised deftly up to the low ceiling. Then he took his covering and vanished through the inner door.

'Think I'll have one of your wines, Mary,' said George, raising his empty tankard.

'Oh, will you?' Mary turned to him. 'Did you come into some money then? You haven't paid your tab in two weeks, George Jarred. Not about to add any more to it, am I?'

'Cold afternoon, though,' George persisted.

'How would you know? Been here hours, you have. Time you went home to your wife, George. You too, William.'

With a deal of grumbling, the two men allowed Mary to drive them out into the wild rain, closing the door fast behind them.

'Now, sir.' She turned to Henry. 'I suspect you'll be wanting food and to stay the night? Not to put too fine a point on it. Can you cover your turn?'

'Yes, Mistress Mary.' Henry patted his jerkin, where a small purse nestled with the few coins he had left. 'If your prices be reasonable.'

'Honest and fair,' she assured him. 'I have a sleeping room for guests upstairs. You could lodge there the night and wait it out.'

He agreed, so Mary went off with logs to light a fire and air the chamber, while Saul reappeared with a platter of bread, cheese and a pat of butter. Henry ate the simple fare as if he hadn't eaten for days, though this wasn't true. The bitter cold had worn him out. The wine was warm, the fire warmer, and his clothes began to steam gently. His belly sated, Henry dozed off where he sat, only dimly aware that Saul was seated opposite him on the far settle, hands folded in his lap, waiting.

Chapter Three

It had grown to full darkness outside when Henry awoke. Mary stood between him and the fire, banking up the logs and rattling the embers to remove the dust. The taproom smelt like washing day, with his clothes, boots and cloak drying. He had no idea how long he'd been asleep. In truth, he had lost track of time altogether that day. The big man, Saul, still sat on the opposite settle with his eyes focused on the flickering flames. Henry's hand strayed to his jerkin, checking for his purse.

'No need for that, sir,' said Mary, so quickly that Henry wondered if she had eyes in the back of her head. 'This may be a poor place compared to some, but it is honest enough. Now, perhaps you might care to share your travels with us? I see you are an army man, and we have little news here.'

'Where is here?'

'Griston, sir. Did you lose your way?'

'Not entirely.' Henry sighed with relief. 'It was so hard to tell once the storm set in. I thought I might have gone off course, but it's not too bad.'

'Where are you heading?' Mary sat on the settle next to Saul, clearly wishing to talk.

'Massingham.' He paused, then added, 'Home.'

'To the north of us, I believe, though I have never gone so far. Watton is our local market, and that suffices for us. Are you on official business?'

Henry shook his head. He considered how much he should keep back and how much he could say. It was hard to know who held what sympathies, even though the war had been officially over for many months following the King's surrender and arrest. He looked past Mary to Saul, who was sitting where he had been when Henry dozed off. The man was staring vacantly at the fire, his eyes held by the flames licking up the logs in the grate.

Mary watched Henry's hesitation, then dug Saul in the ribs. 'Wake up, sleepy. Go and stir the stew for me.'

The man did as he was told with a grunt, going through the door to the kitchen.

'You mustn't worry about my Saul,' Mary assured him. 'God made him simple at birth. Otherwise, I wouldn't still have him with me. He don't say much and thinks less, but he does my bidding, is strong when I need it, and be kind to the animals. My other two sons went off to the fighting.'

'Did they come back?'

'No, neither of them. My eldest died at Edgehill, my second at Cropredy Bridge. Though we're a God-fearing family, it was still a hard burden to bear. At least I have my Saul. He was too simple even for Cromwell to take.'

Henry nodded. It was a common enough story. Families

on both sides had lost their sons, brothers, fathers, even grandfathers.

'Those that survived returned to the village months ago,' continued Mary.

'I stayed on,' said Henry. 'I was attached to the Lord Protector, and we guarded the King.'

'Was? Are you released from the army now, then?'

'You haven't heard the news?'

'It takes a long time to reach us, sir. Have you come from London?'

'Yes. I left four days ago and hoped to be home by tonight.'

'If the storm passes, you can be on your way in the morning. What is this news?'

'It's the King. They executed the King. Five days since.'

Mary looked at him with wide eyes. There was a clatter from the kitchen, and Saul appeared in the doorway, gravy dripping from his fingers. His face, so passive before, was twisted with fear.

'They killed the King?' asked Mary. 'You're sure?'

'I was there. I saw it happen.' Henry's voice grew soft and low. 'I was on duty to keep the crowd from the scaffold.'

'Knew somethin' was wrong,' said Saul. 'I saw the chil'un five nights ago.'

'Hush your noise,' snapped Mary.

But having found his tongue, Saul continued. 'That's bad. Somethin' dreadful always happens when the chil'un be abroad.'

Chapter Four

Mary had driven the wide-eyed Saul back into the kitchen, advising Henry to ignore his ramblings. Closing the door behind her, Henry heard her rebuking the simple man in weary tones.

'You have no sense,' she said. 'Do you want to get accused, like those other poor souls?'

There was a clatter of pots and the sound of heavy footsteps on wooden stairs. Henry knew better than to interfere, so he sat patiently by the fire until the kitchen door creaked open again. Mary returned with another tankard.

'Would you like some more mulled wine, sir?' she asked, picking up the poker and slotting it back into the embers. Henry nodded in agreement, as the wine was indeed as good as George had suggested. 'There's stew for supper if you don't ask where the meat came from.'

'I imagine that might be rabbit,' he smiled. 'I'd be partial to a portion.'

'My own fresh bread too.' Mary plunged the poker to mull

the wine, handed over the tankard, then settled opposite Henry again. 'May I ask you something, sir?'

'I'll answer your questions if I can, if you will satisfy my curiosity in return.'

'About what?'

'The children that Saul spoke of.'

Mary hesitated, then nodded. 'You say that they killed the King. How is that possible? How could they dare? They are only men, and the King is above all of us, second only to God.'

'They tried him in a court of law, although he refused to acknowledge it. Said it was beneath him, besides being illegal to try your own King. Or so my captain told me when he was in his cups. I did not see that, nor would I have understood it if I had.'

'Best leave that sort of thing to our betters,' said Mary.

'Perhaps,' said Henry. 'Though according to some, the point of the war is to stop our betters from hurting us again in the future.'

'I don't pretend to know about these things.'

'Nor do I.' Henry shifted to stretch out his legs.

'And the King?'

'They found him guilty and said he must be executed. There was a platform built outside the Banqueting House in Whitehall. They brought the block and the executioner with his axe.'

'You saw this yourself?'

'They knew a big crowd would gather, and so it did. We were to keep people away from the platform. I never saw the King before that moment, when he stepped out in front of us. But I recognised him from the pictures in the pamphlets.'

Henry became lost in his memory. He gazed into the fire, surprised to find that tears were welling in his eyes.

'Go on, sir,' said Mary.

Henry heaved a sigh. 'I thought they might have to drag him. That he might protest his innocence or shout to the crowd about injustice. I expected it to be like that.'

'But it wasn't?'

'I never saw such dignity in a man, not ever. There was no fear in him, no anger. I thought the crowd might jeer and shout, as they often do at executions at Tyburn. That they might rush forward to attack or even try to save him.'

'They didn't?'

'They stood silent, their faces set like stone, their bodies still as statues. The King gave a simple nod as he walked past Cromwell. No more, no less. When they had fitted him ready for the block, he knelt without assistance, raising his eyes to heaven as the blow fell. There was no sound until his head rolled to stop by the pastor's feet. Then the crowd groaned. Not a cheer or a cry, but a groan. As if some favoured relative had passed to heaven. Many a tear fell as the crowd left the square. Some muttered that it was impossible to kill a king, as he was God on earth to us. As if they couldn't believe the evidence of their own eyes.'

'And you, sir? Did you believe what you saw?'

'The simple truth was a headless body. How could I not believe this? But I thought I saw…' Henry suddenly clamped his mouth shut. He knew that what he thought he'd seen was the workings of a fevered mind. 'No, I saw nothing unusual. I was tired.'

It wasn't possible in Cromwell's new Protestant Commonwealth. He could not possibly have seen the soul of

Charles rise from the quivering body then ascend swiftly heavenwards. Henry had fought in many battles. He had seen many men die, had killed some of them himself. Never once had he seen a soldier's soul depart his earthly body. It was Popish superstition and fear that had clouded his vision.

Mary too had fallen silent, watching the fire as if trying to comprehend what Henry had described. From above their heads, a man's voice drifted down through the wooden ceiling. The tune was plain and mournful. If it was Saul, he had a sweet and clear voice, Henry thought.

'Now it's your turn.'

'Have you heard the tale of the babes in the wood?'

Henry frowned in concentration until a childhood story drifted into his mind.

'Two young children left in the care of their uncle?'

Mary nodded. 'He wished their wealth for himself, but being unable to do the deadly deed with his own hands, he hired horrible ruffians. Told them to take the babes to the wood and do it for him.'

'I remember now. Faced with their innocence, the men couldn't kill them either and abandoned them in the wood to die.'

'Wayland Woods, sir. No more than a mile further along the road to Watton. The hall that he was so greedy to inherit lies between our village and the woods.'

'It's just a story, a tale for the gullible.'

'That is what I believe, but some hereabouts are superstitious. Some say that the babes still walk the earth. Wandering, forever lost, holding hands and searching for help. To see them is a terrible omen.'

Saul's voice ceased its song.

Chapter Five

The rabbit stew was tasty, the bread baked fresh that morning. Sweet wrinkled apples finished the meal. The storm raged on outside. The night sky was masked by the rods of freezing sleet that hammered on the thatch and in the yard. Mary kept the fire well tended, and Henry made no objection when she and Saul sat with him in the taproom to eat their meal. In this new world, ordained by Cromwell, all were citizens, all were equal. Besides, it was surely the warmest room in the house.

'I should check on Oliver,' Henry said as Mary cleared the pots to the kitchen. Saul found two sacks, draped one across his shoulders, waited while Henry did the same, then led him out into the yard.

The sleet had begun to settle, leaving icy shards that made the yard tricky to negotiate. The breath left their mouths in sharply defined white billows. Henry tried to hurry, slid on the half-frozen mud, and was only saved from an undignified fall by Saul, who caught him by the arm. The big man opened the stable door and led Henry in, lighting a safety lantern, which gave off a low light. It was warm inside. The floor was deep in clean straw; fresh hay had been placed in the manger. Oliver had been rubbed down and a dry blanket strapped over his back for comfort. The horse must have been dozing when they approached and threw his head up in alarm until he recognised his master. As Henry patted his neck and fondled his head, the horse settled again, one ear flickering at Saul's soothing murmurs.

'You like animals, Saul?' asked Henry. The big man nodded, looking enviously at the warhorse.

'Wish I had a horse of mine own.'

'Too expensive?'

Saul nodded.

'Earlier on,' Henry watched the big man closely, 'when I spoke of the King, you said that you saw some children five nights ago. What did you mean by that?'

Saul didn't reply at first, gazing at Oliver. Then he began to sing. The voice was barely a breath, but sweet and innocent, like a child's. Oliver leant trustingly against Saul's hand until the man stopped.

'You have a lovely voice. I heard you in the house. Do you sing at church?'

'Sometimes.'

'Is that a hymn? Not one I recognise. Is it a local song, perhaps?'

Saul shrugged and pulled his lips closed. Henry's curiosity was raised. There was something unusual going on here, he felt sure.

'What did your mother mean when she spoke of people

being accused?'

Panic flooded Saul's face. It turned whiter than the sleet outside.

'Did Matthew Hopkins visit the village?'

The big man stepped behind the horse and bent to run his hands down the animal's legs. Henry heard him whisper.

'No chil'un. Nothing.'

Oliver shifted in the straw and nuzzled Henry's hand. He patted the horse. 'We'd better let poor Oliver get his rest.'

With shaking fingers, Saul put out the lantern and drew the sack over his shoulders and head. Henry stepped out into the yard first. Saul followed, pausing to shut the stable door carefully. In the briefest of moments, while he waited for Saul to close the bolts, Henry glanced through the driving sleet towards the lane beyond the yard.

To his horror, he saw two young children standing on the road by the corner of the alehouse. The boy was bigger, presumably older. The girl was gripping the boy's hand. They were poorly dressed for the weather but paid no attention to the wind or sleet. Their cloaks were fastened at the neck, billowing around them, and offered little protection.

Henry was momentarily rigid, unable to focus clearly on the visitors as the sleet drove in painful gusts across the yard. He took a couple of steps towards them, sliding on the ice-bound floor. Saul caught hold of his arm again.

'Look.' Henry turned to face him and pointed to the entrance. 'There are two children out there. We should help them.'

Saul squinted through the storm where Henry indicated, then shook his head.

'No one there, master,' he said. 'Come inside.'

'I saw them, two of them,' Henry insisted. He took a few steps out of the yard and along the lane. The sleet was driven nearly horizontal by the force of the wind. It was difficult to see. He tried to look up and down, the sleet hammering into his face, his view limited to a few yards. It seemed the children had gone. Saul joined him. 'Isn't that them?'

'And if it is,' Saul was shouting above the wind, 'leave well alone, sir.'

'What do you mean? We can't leave two small children out here alone in this weather.'

Holding up his hands to shelter his eyes, Henry scanned the lane until he spotted the pair leaving the village and set off after them.

'They be not real, sir,' called Saul as Henry walked briskly away. 'Only in your head. You won't catch them.'

'Nonsense! Superstition!' Henry shouted over his shoulder, hesitating as the two small figures had vanished again.

'Bad things happen when they visit.'

Henry faced Saul as he came up to join him on the lane. 'Are you saying this is witchcraft?'

'No sir,' Saul stepped backwards in alarm. 'No witches here. All God-fearing folk.'

'Then the children must be real, must be there. They need help.'

Saul hung his head, unable to find an answer. In these uncertain times, men could be accused of witchcraft as easily as women. The memory of the Witchfinder General was still fresh, and the fear he generated still potent.

'Well?'

'No witches here,' said Saul. He crossed himself in the old way, backing away from Henry. 'Come inside, sir.'

'For God's sake. Help me find them.'

'No children. Not here.' Saul sounded frantic. He pulled his sack low over his eyes. 'Leave me be. Nothing, I see nothing.'

Then he turned and ran back to the yard as if the devil were after him.

'Saul! Saul!' Henry shouted angrily. His voice was whipped away by the wind, but he thought he heard an answering voice.

'Saul. Saul.' A child's voice.

Henry spun around and looked along the lane. Beyond the third cottage, he caught a glimpse of two tiny figures climbing the bank. Setting off at a run, repeatedly skidding on the ruined road, Henry tried to overtake the children. Reaching the cottage where he was sure they had turned off the path, he pulled himself up the bank and pushed through the hedge at the top. Its brambles dragged the sack from his shoulders, and he had to tug hard to release it.

Fastening it around his neck with a knot, Henry stumbled across the field beyond, holding his hands above his eyes to try to see. Knowing they couldn't have got far, he plunged on until he reached a belt of trees. Under the branches, the storm was less fierce. Henry paused to catch his breath and surveyed the woods.

Looking back, he could no longer see the lane, the cottages or the alehouse. He must have come too far. Peering into the wood, he caught sight of the children. They walked some distance away, under the protection of the trees. He didn't seem to be gaining on them at all.

'Come back,' he called. But the woods deadened his words, and the children were still walking away.

Setting off at a jog-trot that he felt sure would enable him to overtake the tiny figures, Henry vanished into the woods on his rescue mission.

Chapter Six

The storm raged for three whole days. No more visitors arrived at Mary's alehouse, and Henry did not return. The weather was too vile for anyone to venture forth. Saul brought in what logs they needed to keep the place warm. He looked after Oliver, who rested snug in his stable, content with his treatment. No matter how hard she tried, no word could his mother get from Saul about where Henry had gone or why. If the man had been quiet before, now he was entirely silent. He would not even sing.

When the wind finally dropped, a weak winter sun poked through the clouds. Mary went from cottage to cottage, looking for her guest. He hadn't sought shelter with any of her neighbours. She raised a party, and the villagers began to search the area.

George Jarred found Henry, curled up in a ball beneath an ancient oak in the centre of the wood. He was dead. His body was frozen. No one could have survived outside in that storm for three days. One hand clutched a twisted circle of holly, the berries gleaming like red jewels against his torn and frost rigid jacket.

They carried him back to the alehouse. Mary laid him out for burial once the body had thawed enough to be straightened. But no matter how hard she tried, Mary could not release Henry's fingers from the crown of thorns. The priest came and blessed Henry before they buried him in an unmarked grave in the churchyard.

There was nothing to be found that could identify his home or family. There was no way to notify anyone. In times of war, it was often the case.

Mary kept the few coins that she found in the jacket pocket. Times were hard, food was costly. Saul remained mute for months, except when he looked after Oliver. For he got to keep the magnificent horse, and his dream came true.

Which some people might call witchcraft, as he very well knew.

1841

The one a fine and pretty boy
Not passing five years old;
And the other a girl, more young than he
And fram'd in beauty's mould.
The father left his little son,
As plainly doth appear,
When he to perfect age should come,
Three hundred pounds a year.

And to his little daughter Jane,
Six hundred pounds in gold,
To be paid on the marriage day,
Which might not be controul'd.
But if these children chanc'd to die,
Ere they to age should come,
Their uncle should possess their wealth:
For so the will did run.

Chapter Seven

The wind had been with them ever since they turned out of the Thames estuary. The red-brown sails of the barge had swollen and driven them steadily north along the coast. The cargo of bricks wasn't likely to spoil, like a cargo of food might. Even so, the captain had elected to sail through the night instead of mooring up at one of the Suffolk ports.

'Won't get many more of these easy trips before winter is upon us,' he said to John.

Two men and a boy handled the barge. The latter spent much of the two-day voyage making warm drinks or heating food brought on board by the captain's wife minutes before they had left the Port of London. As their paying passenger, John was included in all these delights. He was also allowed to sleep on one of the two bunks in the cuddy, as the tiny cabin was known.

These barges traded up and down the Thames and east coast, carrying heavy loads more cheaply than horses and carts. The river systems ran deep into the counties from the coastal ports, and it wasn't unusual for them to take a passenger or two.

On the first day out, John simply enjoyed watching the world go by. They were rarely out of sight of the river bank or the coastline. His body and mind both enjoyed the rest, while the sea air eased the tightness in his chest. The second day was fine. After a simple breakfast, he settled on the bench at the rear of the boat and began to sketch in his pad. The captain was at the wheel while his mate and the boy took the chance to rest. He glanced several times at the picture of his barge as it grew under John's expert hand.

'Well, I'll be blowed,' he said. 'Even the rigging is done right. You really caught her there.'

'I love boats,' said John. He lifted his hand and drew an arc on the air. 'And seascapes. They were a speciality of mine for many years.'

'You do this for a living? Can't say I'm surprised. That's good.'

'Not much of a living.' John squinted along the coastline to try and get his bearings. 'Unfortunately. But it is mine, and my son's as well.'

'I thought you was a school teacher. Leastways, that's what the young man said when he came looking for a berth for you.'

'That was Miles, my eldest. We are both teachers, sometimes. It helps to pay the bills.'

'Should you not be at school now, sir?'

'I should.' John sighed and huddled deeper into his coat. The weather was mild, but the breeze that drove them towards Norfolk cut through his clothes. 'I have been unwell, so they have allowed me a little time to myself to recover. I am heading home.'

'Where is home?'

'If anywhere can be called that of the many places I have lived, then it would be where I was born, and my father still is. In Norwich.'

'That'll be why they asked for a barge heading up the Wensum, then. Yarmouth's only an hour or so away.' The captain nodded at the coast. 'May I see that?'

John ripped the sketch of the barge from his pad and handed it over. The captain studied it closely.

'That's as pretty a thing as I've ever seen. Times is hard, you say?'

'Always.'

'Then, if you will allow me to take this for my good lady wife, I dare say it would be acceptable in place of the price of your berth.'

'That would be most kind.' John carefully signed the sketch. It was rather the outcome he had been quietly hoping for. The captain jangled coins in his pocket, returning the half-crowns that John had given him the previous morning.

'Would you take it nice and snug into the cuddy, where it won't get spoiled?'

'Of course. Shall I put it under your pillow?'

'If the boy is up, then yes.'

John climbed down to the cuddy door. Inside he could hear the rattling of metal cups and plates. The boy must be preparing another of those rounds of tea.

'What did you say your name was?' the captain called. 'Then I can tell the wife I met a proper artist.'

'Cotman. John Sell Cotman.'

Chapter Eight

The barge had negotiated the river as high as Thorpe Green, where it moored near a building site for the new railway line. John hoped that the next time he visited Norwich, the much-discussed train service to the city might have been completed.

He said goodbye to the crew and set off to his father's house. The mooring could not have placed him better; the walk took no more than fifteen minutes. It might have been less if he hadn't been burdened with his artist equipment, a bag of clothes and his satchel.

'You should have sent word,' his father said as he welcomed John. 'Could the boy not have come with a message?'

'I didn't think to ask.'

His father sighed. 'You never do. But people are more willing to help than you think. It isn't always an imposition.'

They settled in front of a welcoming fire while his father updated him on the latest news of old friends and the gossip from the Norwich art scene. John's bags had been whisked away to his bedroom by the maid. The housekeeper assured him that the dining room would house his easel and equipment.

'And a fine view of the garden and the green below us, sir,' she assured him. 'Perhaps you may wish to paint that for your father.'

Perhaps he might if he had more time. King's College School had given him a bare two weeks of respite, and then he would have to find another barge to take him back to London. After years of living on a low income, making economies between the sale of each painting and going without food when the children were hungry, the thought made him feel weak. His wife, ever cheerful, always put up with their situation better than he did.

All John wanted to do was settle here in front of the fire and never leave, even though he knew himself to be selfish. There were pains in his chest, and he sometimes had difficulty breathing in the London smog.

'I've made a few arrangements,' John heard his father say. Hoping that it wasn't a round of social engagements, he placed his teacup carefully down on the tray.

'What sort of arrangements?'

'You must not be angry with us.'

John knew he didn't have the energy to be angry with anyone. 'I promise.'

'Ann wrote to me and expressed how worried she was for your health.'

He hadn't known this, but he loved his wife and knew that she would have had the best of intentions. His father continued.

'This respite of yours should be longer.'

'I wish it could be.'

'It can,' his father said. 'Ann has arranged something with Miles. I don't know what. You can stay as long as you need to. She wants you to paint again, to be yourself once more. I have made you an itinerary.'

How like him, John thought. *Always organising things*.

His father went to the small writing bureau and pulled out a list. John scanned down the dates and names, which began with two weeks here in Thorpe with his father. Then there were visits to friends on the north coast at Cromer, in the countryside near Itteringham and Griston and finally back to his father's house. Each visit was for at least a week. In all, it was almost two months.

'What do you think?'

John's heart leapt. He would have the chance to paint again. He could get out into the countryside he loved and stand on the cliffs to watch the sea. He would be able to breathe freely, in the clean air again. If he used the time wisely, he would have a stock of paintings to take back with him and place with his gallery. John smiled.

'Of all things, this is the most wonderful. Thank you.'

Chapter Nine

⁂

Despite the best of intentions, there were times during the trip that John felt as if he were a parcel, being passed from one place to another. Each friendly stay began and ended with a ride in a cart or carriage, all arranged in advance. He found warm rooms and aired beds, plentiful meals and free time to paint or sketch. Although he knew that his father was behind all of it, it was little short of a miracle. The longest distance he undertook was to Griston, which entailed an overnight stay at an inn. It was his last stay before returning to his father, and by now, he was feeling in far better health than when he had arrived.

'My dear fellow,' shouted Joseph Randolph as the local cart pulled up at the front door of Griston Hall. 'Welcome, welcome. We are so pleased to see you.'

Joseph's wife, Hannah, gave the carter a coin and instructed a hovering farmhand to carry John's bags and art equipment inside.

'A painting expedition, no less. We are honoured that you should wish to record our small parish in a work of yours.'

They'd first met at one of John's exhibitions in Norwich. Joseph had purchased a watercolour of fishing boats dragged up on the sands at Great Yarmouth. Later he bought more pictures at various times, and the pair had become good friends.

'See,' said Joseph. He pointed to the row of six pictures, which hung against the oak-panelled walls. 'You are our guest of honour. Do you remember this one? It was my first purchase, and I have never had cause to regret it.'

John examined each painting carefully. He could see how his technique had changed and his skill had grown over the years. These images were all of Norfolk or Norwich, although John had travelled widely when younger and painted wherever he had gone. He thought of the buildings in France, the castles in Wales and the landscapes in the north of England. All of these had sold well on occasion. Joseph's taste remained loyal to his county.

'You'll be needing a rest,' said Hannah as she joined them. 'You must feel free to come and go as you wish.'

'We would love your company, of course,' said her husband. 'Though we understand that your work must take precedence.'

'I would like to do both. Will you show me around your farm and lands?'

It was late afternoon, and the autumn sky was mottled with rosy clouds.

'Red sky at night,' said Joseph.

'Shepherd's delight,' replied John. He longed to fetch his

watercolour box, but it was getting late, and the light would soon be gone.

They made a circuit of the farmyard, Joseph proudly showing off his animals and the latest farm equipment. Hannah kept a pretty herb garden at the front of the house, where they paused to admire the view.

'What are those?' John pointed to distant woodland.

'Wayland Woods. I wouldn't go there if I were you.'

'Why not?'

'It's a place of misfortune. Some say it is haunted.'

John had no belief in ghosts and smiled at this, which Joseph saw.

'Tis no laughing matter. You have heard of the folklore hereabouts, of two babes left to starve in the woods?'

'That's a tale for children and the superstitious, surely?'

'Not here. Those are the very woods where the children were abandoned, and their shades can still be seen from time to time. To see them is bad luck; a death sentence, many claim.'

'Then let us not dwell on such morbid matters.' John turned to face the handsome house. 'Would you like me to make a painting of your home?'

Joseph's face beamed as they returned inside. 'I should like that immensely.

Chapter Ten

The next morning there was a frost on the ground. Autumn had arrived, and the colours were glorious to John. He began by sketching the house from different angles, settling on walking out into the fields between the house and the haunted wood as the best view. He took a stool from Hannah's kitchen and walked further out to find a better perspective. Settling at the best point, he set up his easel and watercolour box. He became so absorbed that he missed the call for lunch until his stomach rumbled and he saw Hannah approaching with a basket.

'I brought some provisions,' she said. 'We did not wish to disturb your work, but I thought you might be hungry.'

'Thank you. I forget the time when I am working.'

She lifted an embroidered cloth to reveal a slice of meat pie, cheese, bread and a bottle of beer. 'Will you help yourself?'

John assured Hannah that there was no need for her to stay. She walked briskly back to her kitchen where, doubtless, other tasks awaited her. The picture of the house was developing to his satisfaction, though it still needed work. Chewing on the slice of pie, John turned to sit facing the other direction.

The colours of the autumn leaves in the woods were magnificent. It was exactly the kind of view that he loved to paint and sometimes was able to sell. Pulling out his sketch pad, he began an outline. It didn't satisfy him. More detail was required.

Taking his pencils and pad, John began to move around the field doing quick studies of different angles. Little by little, he found himself moving closer to the edge of the trees. It was overgrown inside the wood, dense and dark, creating a wonderful contrast to the rust, gold and amber colours of the leaves. John made a dozen or more sketches, each more focused and detailed. His concentration was so great that he hadn't realised the light was fading until he heard Joseph calling.

'John? John, are you there?'

Turning his back on the trees, John could just make out his host standing by the abandoned easel and basket.

'I'm here, Joseph,' he called. The other man scanned the field, failing to find him. John hurried to join him.

'Goodness,' said Joseph. 'My eyes must be failing. You appeared like a phantom.'

They both laughed.

'I'm sorry to have worried you. I was sketching the beautiful trees.'

'Over there? No wonder you have become like a ghost! You haven't seen any, have you?'

'I didn't take you for a superstitious man.' John was surprised.

'Of course not.'

Packing up the equipment, the friends went back to Griston Hall. John showed the painting of the house to the couple.

'It needs a little work,' he said. He held the picture up to consider improvements. 'Will it do as a beginning?'

'Remarkable,' said Joseph.

'Wonderful,' said Hannah.

John sat by the fire to warm himself. The cold had seeped into his bones as the afternoon faded. The year was closing faster than he'd realised. Opening the sketch pad, he leafed through the pictures of the woods. None seemed to be quite the best view until the last one. This final sketch caught the contrast of the intricate tangle of trunks and branches with the dark interior in the dusk. Holding the pad up in the light from the fire, he stared hard at the darkness in the centre of the sketch.

John always drew exactly what he saw in his preparatory work. But he had no recollection of seeing this. It was little more than a suggestion in the movement of his pencil. In the middle of the dark wood, made tiny by the distance, stood a pair of small figures holding hands.

Chapter Eleven

❦

John didn't show the sketch with the two figures to Joseph or Hannah. When he looked at it again the next morning, he could no longer see them.

It must have been a shadow from the firelight, he thought. *The journey must have made me more tired than I realised.*

At first, he worked inside, with the picture of Griston Hall flat on the table so he could work on the finer details. Then, satisfied by his efforts, he left it to dry and went for a stroll, satchel over his shoulder as always.

His feet took him across the field towards the woods, even though he was not conscious of a decision to go there. The place attracted him, though it seemed deserted. A wooden fence at the edge of Joseph's field designed to keep in animals was no barrier to him. Climbing over, John took out his sketch pad and began to draw.

There was a delight for him in the details of twisted branches or moss on the trunks and the sky through the canopy. He could only have been a matter of yards within the boundary when he came across a faint footpath. Flicking back to last night's sketch, it seemed that he was close to where the figures had stood. He still couldn't see them in his pencil workings.

The weather was mild, though the day was grey and overcast. The light along the path was dim, and John was curious.

'If the path runs out,' he murmured, 'I can turn round and follow it back again.'

Sketch pad under his arm, John walked deeper into the trees. The ground was littered with autumn leaves, which muffled the sound of his feet. Occasionally his silent progress startled small birds, who flew away, twittering their fear. Halting to sketch an ancient tree, he turned to glance back along the path he was following.

Somehow, the path had vanished. It was as if the trees had moved, closing the trail behind him.

'Nonsense,' he said loudly. His voice vanished into the gloom. 'It must be there. I've just stepped away from it.'

John turned a full circle and spotted the path again beyond a row of trees. He wondered how he had come to be so far away from it. Striking out across the carpet of dead leaves, keeping the path in view, he struggled through the undergrowth to reach it.

As he stepped out, he saw that it was a different path. The first one was little more than an animal track; this one was a wide ride. Two horses could easily move abreast on it. The width prevented the trees from covering it completely, and what was left of the grey daylight provided little illumination. The wind must have died. Thick trails of mist trickled down from above, weaving between the trunks and along the ride.

John looked in either direction. The fog was growing denser, and he couldn't see the edge of the wood no matter how hard he stared. The place hadn't looked this big from the outside. So which way should he go?

Suddenly the sound of twigs breaking made John turn around. If there was someone else here, they might be able to guide him to the end of the woods. Local people would have permission to gather the dead wood for fires, wouldn't they? They would know the place.

'Hello? Can you help me?'

Silence answered him.

'Is someone there? Can you guide me?'

This time he heard a human sigh. Startled, he spun again, rapidly scanning the surrounding trees. It couldn't have been an animal; they didn't sigh in that way.

'Who's there?' His voice held an edge of fear. 'Come out! I need your help.'

Behind him, there was a rustle in the dead leaves. He turned for the third time. Yards along the ride, he glimpsed something. Perhaps it was grey, and perhaps it was white. It might be an animal or a poor farm worker not wanting to be seen. No, it was too small for an adult. Ice ran down his spine.

'You don't believe in ghosts,' he reminded himself. Raising his voice, he shouted, 'Please don't be afraid of me. Can you wait?'

The mist was swirling closer, reducing his line of sight by the minute. John set off after whatever he had seen. It was his best hope.

He hurried along a faint path that led away from the ride. Under the cover of the trees, it grew colder. The mist formed a sheen of damp on his clothes, which soaked through to his skin. It grew so thick that John couldn't see more than a few feet in front of him. He shivered as he strode on until he reached a break in the trees.

The mist thinned a little, and peering around, John tried to get his bearings. Was that someone ahead of him? Were those shapes people? Or a trick of the fog and fading light?

'Wait for me! Please help me!'

Panic overwhelmed him, and he set off at a run. But this was his undoing. John had undertaken this journey for the sake of his health. Now, as he ran, his chest tightened and his breathing became laboured. Nor was the activity warming him as it should. Shivers wracked him as his progress slowed. Finally, he stopped, unable to go further. He sat down on the cold, damp ground and leant against a tree.

'Help me,' he called. But his voice was as tired as his body; it didn't carry.

Ahead of him, he heard twigs snapping, feet running. Or was it hooves trotting? Raising his eyes to search the encroaching wall of mist, John caught a glimpse of something tawny red. Whatever was moving broke out into a wild run. Hooves galloped away into the distance. He must have been following a deer.

He slid sideways onto a pile of leaves and tried to pull his coat around him as he drifted in and out of sleep. The night was closing in. He had no idea where he might be.

Chapter Twelve

John had no notion of how long he lay there. It was the barking of dogs that brought him back to full consciousness. His limbs were stiff; he could barely move. At some point he had curled up, his frozen fingers gripping the satchel, which was acting as a pillow. Now a friendly dog's nose was rooting in the earth around him, urging him to sit up. The animal barked an excited volley. A warm tongue was licking his face.

'Pip! Pip! Where are you?'

Someone was calling the animal away, but it refused to leave him, barking again in response to its name. John recognised the voice with gratitude. It was Joseph. His friend lumbered through the undergrowth, followed by a second dog and two farmhands. He dropped to his knees next to John.

'Thank God, we've found you. You've been missing for hours.'

Blankets were laid on him. Pip was encouraged to lie next

to him for warmth. The farmhands ran off, returning as quickly as they could with a wattle panel. Lifting John carefully onto it, they carried him through the fog back to the hall. The men had no difficulty in finding their way out of the trees.

The dogs ran around barking excitedly as they burst into the kitchen. Hannah was waiting for him. She gently removed his satchel from his cold fingers and led him to the fireside.

'Thank you,' said John. His words were barely audible over the chattering of his teeth. The farmhands nodded and tucked the coins Joseph gave them into their pockets before leaving.

The couple stripped the worst of John's soaking clothes and wrapped him in warm blankets. Pip settled by his feet in front of the grate. A mug of hot milk, laced with something alcoholic, was raised to his lips. Slowly, sense and feeling returned.

'You should rest now,' said Hannah. 'I've got the warming pan ready for your bed, and the fire in your room is lit.'

'My bag,' murmured John. He reached with chapped fingers towards the satchel on the table.

'No need to worry about that,' said Joseph. 'It will be safe enough when I put it with your other work.'

'I need my bag,' John insisted, becoming agitated.

Hannah brought the satchel to him. The leather was as cold and soaked as he had been. Opening the flap, he pulled out the sketch pad. The cardboard cover was wet but not soaked. The papers at each end were damaged; those further inside were safe. With a groan of frustration, his unwilling fingers could not turn the pages. The satchel slipped from his knee to the floor.

'Let me help you,' said Hannah. 'You wish to see if your work is safe?'

John nodded. She laid the pad on his lap and began to open each page that she could, flipping them with dexterity. He watched each page avidly. There were sketches from various stops on his journey, and his livelihood might depend on making full watercolours from these ideas.

As Hannah reached the most recent ones, John held up a shaking hand. She turned the pages more slowly until she reached the one he was looking for. He pointed, and she stopped turning. Bending forward, he tried to look more closely. His tired joints made him groan.

'Is this the one you wish to see most?' Hannah asked. She lifted the pad, tilting it towards the light from the candle on the table next to John.

In the dark interior of the wood, in the centre of the sketch, stood two small children. They had returned to the picture. This time they were quite distinct and much closer: a boy and a girl, dressed in old-fashioned clothes. John dropped the sketch pad to the floor.

Chapter Thirteen

John was confined to his bed for two days. Hannah and Joseph fussed around him, bringing anything he wanted except the tools of his trade.

'Don't you be worrying about painting or drawing,' insisted Hannah. 'Your things are all safe where you left them. No one will dare to touch them.'

The first morning he tried to get up, his legs felt distinctly wobbly. With Joseph's help, he put on a dressing gown and went down to the parlour. His work was exactly where Hannah had promised that it would be. A fire warmed the room. He settled by it while his hosts brought tea and fresh bread to toast.

'I must go on with my work,' said Joseph. He passed the toasting fork to John, a delicious slice of lightly browned bread balanced on the end. 'The fog that caught you has only lifted this morning. We must check the animals.'

'You are both so kind to me.'

'Nonsense. What else are friends for? Will you rest here a while?'

'I promise.'

'If you feel able, perhaps you could sign the picture for us.'

Joseph waved at the table where John's painting of Griston Hall lay surrounded by the rest of his sketches.

'Of course.'

John listened as Joseph set off with the shepherd and the two dogs who had saved him in the woods. Hannah returned to her kitchen, and peace descended on the parlour. Finishing his breakfast, John poured another dish of tea. It was an expensive commodity that should not be wasted. Refreshed and feeling stronger, he stood at the table.

He gathered up the sketches of the house first.

Would his hosts like these as well? he wondered.

Placing them in order, he inspected them one by one. The last sketch was almost as good as his final painting, despite its rapid execution. He studied it with a smile. The house filled most of the space on the page, Hannah's pretty garden before it. He hadn't recollected drawing a figure there. On closer inspection, he could see that it was Hannah cutting herbs.

In which case, he decided, *I shall give Hannah this one with the final painting.*

There were no figures in any of the others. John pulled the sketch pad open, leafing through the pages until he reached the one he searched for. The two figures that he thought should be in the dark centre were not there. His mind must be playing tricks on him. Getting trapped in the woods, falling asleep and becoming so cold; all this must have upset his judgement. It was just a sketch of the woods, with a path leading into a dark patch under the trees.

John found his pen and a pot of ink. Settling on a chair, he pushed aside all the sketches except the one for Hannah. Then he placed the finished painting next to it. Taking care not to dribble ink, he signed the watercolour and set it to one side. Then with equal care, he signed the lower corner of the sketch.

'No sand,' he said to himself. Sprinkling sand on the signatures would dry them more quickly. 'Perhaps in Joseph's bureau.'

The desk stood against the oak panelling, underneath the gallery of John's work. Pulling gently at the lid, he soon found and extracted the pounce pot. A draft of cold air disturbed him as he reached the table. The sooner he had finished this task, the quicker he could return to sitting by the fireplace.

First, he sprinkled the sketch, then he counted to ten before blowing the spare sand into the grate. Reaching for the watercolour, his hand faltered. He was adamant that there were no figures in this picture, not even when he had signed it a moment before. But now, there was a face at an upstairs window.

John leant over to look more closely. It was a man. The face was scowling, the corners of his mouth and eyes wrinkled with hatred. He appeared to be leaning on a window ledge and was staring into the garden below. Had someone been playing tricks with his picture? Would he have to do it over? That would be a shame, as it was good work. Nor did he recognise the face. It certainly wasn't his host or any of the farmhands that he had met during his stay. He leant over to look even more closely.

The angry face turned and looked directly at him.

With a cry of terror, John shot backwards, scattering ink and sand everywhere and smashing the chair as he crashed to the floor.

Chapter Fourteen

Hannah said later that she heard the noise and rushed to help. Calling for the kitchen maid, they lifted John onto the chair by the fire. The distinctive scent of smelling salts revived him. A cold sweat covered his body, and he was shaking. The maid was cleaning up the spilt ink.

'I knew you should not have left your room today,' said Hannah. 'It is too soon.'

'I fear you are right,' John replied. 'I am exhausted. Do you think you can help me back to my bed?'

Hannah smiled at the maid, who looked a strong and capable girl. 'We shall try.'

'Do one thing for me first. Bring me the painting I have done for you and the sketch that I signed.'

'The ink fell to the floor. Your work is not damaged.'

'Even so, I would like to see it.'

She brought the two pictures. Barely able to hold them in his shaking hands, John inspected the pencil sketch first. It was as he knew it should be. He handed it to Hannah.

'This is for you. You can see yourself in it.'

'Why, thank you.' Hannah looked at the picture and nodded. 'So I am.'

Fearfully, John looked at the watercolour. The face was still at the window, but the image was faint. If this had been real, you might have thought that the man had stepped back inside the room and into shadow.

'For you and Joseph,' he said. 'I am sorry about the man at the window. I have no recollection of putting him there.'

He tried to laugh, but his voice wouldn't obey him. His throat felt wretchedly sore. Hannah wrinkled her brow and accepted the picture. She studied it closely.

'Which window?'

'At the top on the left. I think it must be your room now, but that isn't Joseph.'

'Are you sure?'

She held the picture out for him to look at. The face was gone. John felt tired enough to cry.

'I must be mistaken,' he said. 'You are right; I need more rest.' He returned wearily to his room.

His words worried Hannah so much that she told Joseph of them when he returned. They examined the painting but could find no sign of a face in any of the windows.

'I fear that he is sicker than we thought,' said Joseph. 'His father should know. If I leave now, I can be there by midnight.'

John did not hear Joseph's departure; he was deeply asleep. His dreams swirled with the mist and the forest, the two children in their strange clothes and the face of the man in the window.

He began to cough, and his chest tightened. His body

changed from freezing cold to burning hot several times in each hour. Sometimes he was aware that Hannah was bathing his forehead with cooling water. Other times he felt her slip the warming pan under the bedcovers for a few moments. He found it hard to catch a decent breath. Most of the time, he turned and turned again, unable to settle.

Finally, the visions receded, and he slept quietly. When he woke again, his father sat by his bed.

'John? Have you come back to us?' His father sounded relieved.

Blinking in the morning sunlight, which glittered through the window, John took in his surroundings.

'I have had such awful dreams.'

'You have been very ill. I thought that we might lose you. Hannah has been a tower of strength.'

'But my work. I saw two children in my sketch and a man at the window in my painting. I didn't put them there. I didn't dream them, did I? Are they still there? I must see it.'

By the time his father brought the pad and painting, John was sitting up in bed with a tray of nourishing soup waiting on the bedside table. John held out his hands.

The watercolour was free of figures or faces. The pencil drawing showed only a footpath into a dark wood.

'I was so sure. Two children and a man.'

'You have had a bad fever,' said his father. 'No wonder that it might make you see things that you did not recognise. Don't you think, Hannah?'

'I think you have been listening to my husband's nonsense,' she said. 'It's just a story, used to frighten children into behaving well.'

'Ah, that would make sense. Just the old ghost story, eh, Hannah?'

With a sigh, John gave Hannah the two pictures. He accepted the bowl of soup. 'I dare say you are right.'

Chapter Fifteen

John stayed longer at Griston Hall than they'd originally intended. It meant that he had to cut short his last visit with his father in Thorpe, and the painting he had begun there wasn't finished to his satisfaction. A barge heading back to London was found, a passage purchased, and his belongings packed up.

It was a bright late autumn morning when his father saw him off on his journey home. John was wrapped up against the sea winds, which would help them back to the Thames. He hugged his father goodbye and stowed his things in the cuddy with the boy's help. He knew that his health was no better than when he had arrived. That brief few weeks of travel, rest and creativity had been the best of it. His chest was tight despite the fresh sea air, and he dreaded returning to his duties at the school in London. But it would be wonderful to see his family again, and his portfolio was bursting with new work that might make an exhibition for him. His duty was to return.

Afterwards, Joseph felt guilty that John had become ill while staying with them at Griston Hall.

'I shouldn't have told him about the story.'

'He's a grown man,' said Hannah. 'John made his own decisions, followed his own desire to sketch in the woods.'

'I still do not see the face he spoke of,' Joseph replied as he hung the newly framed painting of Griston Hall at the end of his row of Cotman watercolours.

'Because it was never there,' Hannah assured him, admiring the picture. 'Don't they look fine?'

'And yours?'

'I love it.'

They framed Hannah's sketch, which she had them place in their bedroom, next to where she slept. Not many people would see it there, unlike her husband's collection.

It was probably a good thing, she later decided. Most often, when she looked, Hannah saw herself as John had drawn her, bent at the waist, cutting herbs for the kitchen. But once or twice a year, the picture changed. Perhaps it was a trick of the light, or maybe her eyes were deceiving her as she grew older.

On those days, she was handing a posy to two small children who stood with her amongst the flowers. They were holding hands.

1899

The parents being dead and gone,
The children home he takes,
And brings them strait unto his house,
Where much of them he makes,
He had not kept these pretty babes
A twelvemonth and a day
But for their wealth he did devise
To take their lives away.

He bargain'd with two ruffians strong,
Who were of furious mood,
That they should take these children,
And slay them in a wood.
Then told his wife, and all he had,
He did the children send
For to be brought up in fair London
By one that was their friend.

Chapter Sixteen

The Reverend Frederick Collings and his wife, Matilda, seemed very fond of children. It was such a shame, said the people of the village of Griston, that they had none of their own. Or to be precise, none left alive. When the vicar had first taken on the parish almost twenty years before this Christmas of 1899, the couple had brought their two beautiful young babes with them. A son aged five and a daughter aged three. Smallpox had claimed them, as it claimed so many others that year. Now they lay in a quiet grave, not far from the vestry door of St Peter and St Paul's church in the heart of the village.

Some said that the heart of Matilda Collings lay with them. The couple had not been blessed with any other babies, and slowly the young wife had become a quiet, middle-aged woman who dedicated herself to good works amongst the poor. Especially the children. She had personally selected the pleasant master who taught in a single-room village school. Under her supervision and with her regular assistance, the children learnt to read and write and work their numbers. All was done with encouragement, not punishments. Matilda would not allow the use of canes or switches, or slippers to chastise the tardy or the rude. The villagers loved her for it.

The same could not be said for the vicar. Although he appeared to approve of his wife's assisting with the school, he was also bellicose and loud, given to preaching on the merits of knowing your place and keeping to it. More recently, his Sunday sermons had included a lengthy mention about the glory of the new war in South Africa. He finished with an exhortation for local young men to join the army and support the cause.

What Matilda thought of these perorations the villagers did not like to ask, though many a whispering gossips had their own opinions. She always sat alone in her designated pew during the services, with her head bent over her hymnal.

'Like chalk and cheese,' said one village matron to another, as they left the morning service a few days before Christmas.

'Mrs Gedge says he's just as loud at home,' said the second. 'And she should know.'

'Poor lady.'

They wandered away down the village street amongst the rest of the retreating parishioners. Being farm labourers and working folk, they didn't receive a leaving attention from the Reverend Collings. He preferred to expend his time on Lord and Lady Randolph, who had descended from their London home to Griston Hall for the festive holidays.

'Delighted to see you this morning,' the vicar said. 'A rare honour for us. Are you here for Christmas?'

'Our townhouse is being renovated,' replied Lord Randolph. 'We decided to visit our country cottage for a change.'

'Griston Hall is hardly a cottage,' said Collings.

'Perhaps not.' Lord Randolph shook the vicar's hand once only, the least he could do without seeming rude. His wife leant on his arm, shivering in her fine silk gown, the fur collar to her coat barely fulfilling its office.

'Cold in there this morning,' Lord Randolph continued.

'Sadly, yes,' said Lady Randolph. 'However, your sermon was most uplifting, Mr Collings. May I ask where your wife is at present?'

'Tidying up the hymn books,' said Collings. 'Unless she has already gone to see to my lunch.'

'I had hoped to speak to her,' she said. 'Perhaps you would be kind enough to ask her to call on me this afternoon if she isn't too busy.'

'Women's work, eh?' said Lord Randolph with a smile.

'Indeed. Shall we go?'

The vicar dropped his head in acknowledgement. The wealthy couple walked along the path to the front gate, where their carriage waited for them. Pausing only until the couple climbed in, Collings stalked back inside the church to change. His wife was piling hymn books on a small table near the font.

'Her ladyship wants to see you this afternoon,' he said to Matilda as he passed. 'Don't know why.'

Matilda looked up in surprise. The Randolphs rarely visited Griston Hall, as it was by far the smallest of their three homes. When they did, it was usually her husband who was summoned to keep Lord Randolph company when the latter grew bored. Griston Hall sounded grand, but in practice, it was little more than a glorified farmhouse and very different from the large Belgravia townhouse that Matilda understood to be their London home.

Collings marched down the aisle to the vestry, calling over his shoulder, 'You'd better put on your best dress before you go over there. You look so dowdy. And make sure you don't let me down with your behaviour. Will our lunch be ready in time?'

Outside in the cold air, Matilda's teeth began to chatter, despite her warm wool coat. An earth footpath led from the church porch, past the vestry door and across the churchyard to the rectory garden's small rear gate. The ground was frozen solid. She could feel it through the soles of her boots and wondered how the poorer children of the parish managed with their threadbare clothes and hand-me-down boots.

Matilda paused on the path in front of the graves of her two children. She could never pass without stopping to offer a silent prayer that they were with God. Some kind soul had left a spray of holly with bright red berries on the grass mound in front of the headstone.

Turning to see if there was anyone to thank for the gesture, it seemed that almost all of the village families were already far along the lane. The carriage to Griston Hall was out of sight, though she could still hear the clip of the horses hooves on the frozen road. Almost all. In the gateway to the lane at the edge of the churchyard, Matilda could see two small children, standing silently, holding hands.

They don't look old enough to be left on their own, she thought. *Where on earth are their parents?*

She turned to look up and down the lane for the errant family who must have misplaced two of their number, half expecting to see an embarrassed mother hurrying back to collect the young pair. There was no one. When she looked back at the gateway, the children were gone. She heard her husband rattling the keys in the vestry door, and knowing that he would be wanting his meal, Matilda hurried fearfully along the path to the rectory garden, all thought of the two lonely youngsters driven from her head.

Chapter Seventeen

Mercifully, Mrs Gedge, the housekeeper, had anticipated that lunch would need to be ready the moment the Reverend Collings returned from the church. The hoar frost that lay on the trees and lawn in the vicarage garden had been sufficient warning that the church would be extremely cold, despite the warming pipes that had been installed several years ago. It was the duty of one of the churchwardens to go in on such mornings and light the boiler in the base of the belfry tower. The warm water, which was subsequently pumped around the pipes underneath some pews, gave a select number of parishioners a little help to fight off the chill. The high vaulted roof and stone-lined building sucked the heat away, no matter how much coal they fed through the boiler's door.

Mrs Gedge also knew full well that Mr Collings was not above giving Mrs Collings a slap if things were not in order. He was always careful to leave no marks that could be seen, but Mrs Gedge had heard enough to know, and so she always ensured their meal was waiting to be served the moment the vicar and his wife entered the dining room.

A large fire was pumping out heat near to the vicar's chair. Mrs Gedge quietly escorted Matilda into the room before removing her outdoor coat, and assured her that the meal was ready. At least Matilda had a few moments alone with the blaze to warm herself before her husband strode across the garden to the house.

'What does Lady Randolph want with you?' he asked Matilda as they began to eat the heart-warming stew that constituted their midday meal.

'I'm sure I can't imagine,' said Matilda. Nor could she.

'See to it that you behave with decorum. Or I shall want to know why.'

'I shall do my very best.'

'That is rarely good enough,' declared the vicar. 'I think I shall accompany you. The walk will do me good.'

There was little point in arguing. His curiosity would be too strong to stay away. What Lady Randolph would think of his imposition would be another matter. Certainly, the butler who opened the door to them at Griston Hall seemed mildly surprised to see the vicar with his wife.

'Lady Randolph is in the sitting room, Mrs Collings,' he said. 'She is expecting you.'

If the vicar's appearance put out Lady Randolph, she was far too well bred to show it. Matilda kept her eyes lowered in submission.

'What a delightful surprise,' said Lady Randolph. The vicar bowed slightly, but she beckoned the butler forward before Mr Collings could attempt to sit down. 'Do you know where my husband is?'

'I believe he is in the gun room with the gamekeeper, my lady.'

'Would you let him know that the vicar has been so kind as to call?'

As the butler left, Lady Randolph gestured gently to an armchair on the opposite side of the warm fire and encouraged Matilda to sit down, leaving the vicar standing with ill-grace in no-man's land between the door and the sofa.

'I'm sure you would prefer to help with the planning of the Boxing Day shoot than listen to ladies' gossip,' she said. Mr Collings was forced to agree. When the butler returned with Lord Randolph's invitation, he had no further reason to stay in the room.

Matilda knew it would annoy him beyond measure and could only admire the deftness with which he had been dismissed. Lady Randolph opened a polite conversation about the weather and the respective parties' health until the housemaid had delivered a tea tray replete with tiny confectioneries.

'Milk?' asked Lady Randolph. She poured the tea and loaded a plate with a selection of delicacies that she passed to Matilda before settling back in her chair. 'Now we are alone, we can talk. You must be wondering why I have asked you here?'

Matilda nodded, sipping her tea politely and waiting.

'Do you still hold your annual children's party?'

'Oh yes, ma'am.'

'How many children attend?'

'At least one from each poor family,' explained Matilda. 'I see them at school and choose them that way.'

'And is the school adequate for the current needs of the village?'

'To be truthful, we could help the children more easily if they were not all in one room. They vary so much in age; it is often difficult for the younger ones to keep up with the lessons.'

'They must attend between the ages of five and thirteen; is that correct?'

'Yes, my lady.' Matilda couldn't see where this conversation was going.

'You and I share a misfortune, do we not?'

Lady Randolph's daughter had also died young, and she lay in the family tomb in an exclusive London church. Matilda looked down shyly.

'I have been thinking of our losses recently,' said Lady Randolph. 'They changed us both, did they not? I came to dote on my son and my husband while you take care of the village children. It seems to me that you do rather more good than I.'

'I'm sure I couldn't say,' said Matilda, still at a loss.

'You may not be aware, but we are about to become grandparents.'

Matilda offered congratulations, which were accepted with a smile. The Randolphs' son was grown up, worked in London and was, presumably, married. A grandchild would undoubtedly be very welcome.

'This happy prospect has made me reflect on our good fortune,' Lady Randolph said. 'In fact, you could say that it has turned me into something of a radical.'

'Radical?' Matilda was horrified. Lady Randolph smiled at her reaction.

'I intend to ensure that all my grandchildren, whether male or female, receive a full and proper education. Education is so important, isn't it?'

'Extremely.' This was one thing they could definitely agree on.

'My reflections have also made me realise that many of our workers' children are less fortunate. Accordingly, I have decided that I shall undertake something for them too. And this is what I would like to enlist your help with.'

Matilda's eyes opened wide with surprise. Lord and Lady Randolph were good landlords in as much as their tenants' cottages were kept repaired, and work was fairly paid. But they had previously shown little interest in the villagers.

'When do you hold your children's party?'

'On Boxing Day,' said Matilda.

'Do you still provide the children with presents?'

'Indeed, my lady. And a small parcel to take home to their families, with food treats to be shared with those who we cannot accommodate in the vicarage.'

'Space is the issue?'

'Partly,' said Matilda. She was reluctant to add that money was the main issue. The party was funded from savings she managed to make from the housekeeping and her dress allowance. It never went as far as Matilda would like.

'As it will soon be the new millennium, I would like this year to be a little more ambitious.' Lady Randolph set down her cup and saucer, leaning forward to speak with enthusiasm. 'I would like the party to be held here, in Griston Hall. I want every child aged twelve or less to attend. To be fed royally and given a present of a piece of warm clothing. What do you send to the families?'

Matilda's head was spinning. 'Usually, a slab of Christmas fruit cake, a wheel of cheese and a few sweets.'

'Then we shall add something for each child too old to attend, and their parents too. I will provide the funds, but you must help me plan it. In fact, I can't possibly manage it without you.'

Lady Randolph smiled at Matilda's blushes.

'There is something else I would like to do. When the new century begins, we shall endow the village school with another classroom and all necessities. I hope you will also help me with this project?'

Matilda agreed that she would be delighted. It was years since anyone had valued her opinion, and Lady Randolph's plans depended on her. The only problem would be her husband's reaction.

Chapter Eighteen

Matilda soon discovered that Lady Randolph was a fearsome organiser. As there were only three days until Christmas Eve to make the arrangements, they had begun as soon as they had finished their tea. They drew up a list of all the families in the village that Matilda felt could be invited if money were no object.

'Who does that leave out?' asked Lady Randolph.

'Not many,' said Matilda. 'There is a handful of old people. Pensioners, if you will.'

'Make a separate list of them, and I will arrange hampers for them. Anyone else?'

'Just the blacksmith, the innkeeper and the shopkeeper.'

'Do you think they would feel too proud to be included?'

'More likely that they would feel offended at being left out,' said Matilda. Lady Randolph laughed.

They counted up the lists, and it represented a serious number of gifts and hampers of food.

'I do not think,' said Lady Randolph reflectively, 'that we

can furnish all of this locally. We should go to Norwich and see what we can do there. Are you free tomorrow?'

Matilda said that she was. 'The cakes I make myself. They are already waiting to be distributed. I normally buy the cheese and the sweets from Mr Wade; he will be expecting me.'

'Then order double your normal amount, and put it on our account.' She rang for a servant and requested the attendance of the housekeeper.

Unlike Mrs Gedge, a local woman with a warm heart and a keen eye, this housekeeper travelled with the family from their London home. If she was honest, Matilda found the woman intimidating. She accepted Lady Randolph's instructions without a murmur or flicker of movement on her face. This party would cause her a lot of extra work, Matilda realised, but the housekeeper wordlessly opened the tiny notebook that hung from her chatelaine and began to make notes. By the time Mr Collings and Lord Randolph joined them and a fresh tray of tea had been provided, the three women had a plan of action.

'Well, my dear?' asked Lord Randolph. He settled on the sofa to drink his tea.

'All is settled,' replied his wife. 'We have already begun.'

'How delightful.'

'We will need to go to Norwich tomorrow.'

'Carriage to Watton first thing, then a train?'

Mr Collings looked on, mystified. He glowered at his wife, clearly angry that she knew something he did not for once. Matilda turned herself slightly in her chair so that she couldn't see him too well, determined to enjoy her few moments amid the secret and under the protection of Lady Randolph.

Of course, he grilled her as they walked home. They were barely out of earshot of the front door before he demanded an explanation. On the pretext of pulling her arm through his, as a well-bred gentleman would do, he pinched her arm spitefully and crushed her hand in his. When he heard the plan, he laughed derisively.

'Good, for once I shan't be called upon to try and control those noisy youngsters,' he said. 'I'm grateful that they aren't making a mess in my house this year. Lord Randolph has invited me to go on the Boxing Day shoot with his friends. That will be far more enjoyable.'

Chapter Nineteen

Matilda and Lady Randolph enjoyed a long day in Norwich. They spent a great deal of time in various shops in the morning, ordering invitation cards and presents for the children. After lunch in a charming corner tea house, they went to a huge department store. Lady Randolph ordered fabric lengths for the mothers, neckerchiefs for the fathers and a piece of warm, ready-made clothing for each child in the village. She added lengths of ribbon to tie up parcels and pretty linen handkerchiefs to be knotted up once filled with sweets.

Matilda didn't dare to ask how much it all cost. The shop's manager sat them in a private area, provided them with a pot of tea and fussed around them for nearly two hours. They arrived home late, and Matilda sat exhaustedly listening to her husband's complaints about having to spend the day on his own.

'You are neglecting your wifely duties,' he grumbled. 'Do I have to remind you of them?'

'Of course not.' Matilda kept her tone humble. 'I hope I am a good wife to you. Lady Randolph requested my help, which reflects well on you.'

Mr Collings bent over the chair where Matilda sat, head lowered and hands folded in her lap. He gripped her chin with bony fingers, forcing her to look at him.

'Do you understand what will happen if you embarrass me?'

Matilda fixed her gaze over his shoulder to avoid the look in his eyes. He rattled her shoulder with his other hand. His grip on her jaw tightened.

'Answer me.'

'I understand.'

'Bedlam awaits if you disobey me.' The next morning, Matilda headed through the village to the shop at the end of the street, accompanied by Mrs Gedge. The housekeeper had been appraised of the plan and enthusiastically volunteered her services in any way required. The shopkeeper was startled at Matilda's order but assured her that it would be delivered to Griston Hall as soon as possible. Three times that day, the two women saw the pony and trap from the railway station clatter down the lane loaded with parcels from the shopping trip.

In the afternoon, Matilda and Mrs Gedge walked to Griston Hall, leaving the Reverend Collings to write his Christmas Day sermon in his study. The morning room at the hall was filled with parcels, which Lady Randolph and her housekeeper were already unpacking.

'Do you have the list?' Lady Randolph asked when Matilda joined them. She seemed carried away with enthusiasm at the project, and if Matilda had expected all the hard work to fall to herself and Mrs Gedge, then she was wrong. Pausing only for an occasional visit to the tea tray, the four women opened, folded, distributed and counted out the goods until each pile represented the presents for an individual family.

Matilda found that she became adept at portioning out the sweets and tying them up in the handkerchiefs. They bundled the parcels together and wrapped the piece of dress fabric around it. The two housekeepers tied each bundle with a length of hair ribbon while Matilda and Lady Randolph wrote out labels. Finally, the two housekeepers went back to their duties, while Matilda helped Lady Randolph address the invitations, which she gave to the butler to distribute around the village.

'Leave no one out,' she said, handing him Matilda's list. 'Have the hampers for the elderly arrived?'

'In the pantry, my lady,' he said. She gave him the second list. 'First thing on Boxing Day morning, then.'

'A good day's work. I think,' said Lady Randolph. The pair surveyed the table loaded with gifts. 'The villagers will be surprised and pleased.'

Matilda nodded shyly. 'I hope they will. I should get home.'

Lady Randolph laid her hand gently on Matilda's arm. 'May I ask you something?'

'I don't think we have missed anyone.' Matilda couldn't think of any other question.

Lady Randolph traced a finger along Matilda's jawline. 'Where have these come from?'

'Nowhere.' Matilda's hands shot up in front of her face in panic. 'I caught myself. I don't know.'

'I see.' Lady Randolph looked at her keenly. 'Would you like me to order the carriage to take you back to the vicarage?'

Matilda declined, wanting to get a moment's peace before returning to her husband. If he suspected that his actions of last night had left a mark that could be seen by someone else or that anyone had asked about them, it would be the worse for Matilda. The walk would settle her emotions.

It was bitterly cold, and frost was forming on the grass in the churchyard as Matilda went to say a short prayer at her children's grave. The night was clear. An almost full moon and a star-strewn sky made it easy to see where she was going. Turning the corner of the church, she suddenly stopped. To her surprise, she could see the same two children she had first noticed on Sunday. They were walking past the vestry door, hand in hand. Matilda thought she knew all the village children, and it irked her that she didn't recognise the pair. What on earth were they doing out here on such a cold evening and after dark?

The tiny figures continued across the graveyard until they reached the yew tree in the corner. The tree was nearly as old as the church building itself, Mrs Gedge had once told her. Its girth certainly indicated great age, and its branches hung over many a grave and into the lane outside, obscuring her view. The cold air made Matilda's breath stream out in wispy vapours as she stood wondering what to do. If she had missed two children, they would be without presents at the party, and it would be a shame for anyone to feel disregarded. But she couldn't for the life of her place who they belonged to. It wouldn't do, she decided. Everyone had to be included; she just needed to know who they were.

With sudden determination, she cut across the grass to the tree, frost crunching under her boots, leaving a clear trail to mark her passage. When she got there, the children had already gone. She walked around the tree, peered down the dark lane, checked behind the nearest gravestones without success. Matilda retraced her path to the vestry door. The strange thing was that although she could see her footsteps in the frost, there was no trace of the children.

My search must have obscured their tracks, she thought, as she arrived back at the vestry door.

Pausing to offer her usual prayer, Matilda saw a fresh offering of greenery on her children's grave. The tiny needles and jewel-red berries of a newly grown branch of the yew lay sparkling on the grass near the headstone.

Chapter Twenty

Christmas Day was always a trial to Matilda. While the entire village enjoyed the carols, she stood mouthing the words and worrying about their dinner. If this meal, above all others, had any fault in it, then Mr Collings would find it and blame her. With some trepidation, she had bought her husband a book from the department store in Norwich. It sat wrapped and waiting with a box of his favourite cigars to be presented before the meal. He rarely bothered to get her anything, and if he did, it would be practical and not personal.

When the service ended, the congregation hurried away, keen to reach their own Christmas feasts. Matilda collected the hymn books, as usual, stacking them on the table near the font.

'Merry Christmas, my dear,' said Lady Randolph. She must have come back inside while Matilda was busy. 'I hope you don't mind me taking the liberty.'

She placed a parcel into Matilda's hands, then leant

forward and kissed her on the cheek. Matilda blushed, not least because she had not imagined such a gesture and hadn't bought anything for Lady Randolph.

'Until tomorrow morning,' said her ladyship. The pair left the church together. Mr Collings could barely conceal his frown when he saw them. Matilda knew his pride would be pricked if she seemed to be forming a friendship with Lady Randolph when Lord Randolph offered no such compliment to him.

She bobbed her head, kept her eyes down and walked out of the porch before he could say anything. Clutching her parcel, Matilda strode along the path, pausing briefly to say her regular prayer. This morning, someone had laid a sprig of mistletoe beside the branch of yew. It hadn't been her, and, surely, it hadn't been her husband. She hurried on to the house, where Mrs Gedge was waiting. Without a word, she took off her coat and hastened upstairs. Her husband usually kept to his own bedroom or study these days, for which Matilda was grateful. Her bedroom was a sort of sanctuary. Anxiously glancing out of the window across the garden at the churchyard, Matilda hid the parcel under the mattress. Rushing back downstairs, she waited in the dining room until Mr Collings returned.

His mood was triumphal. Lord Randolph had not only reminded him of the invitation to the Boxing Day shoot but had also presented him with a bottle of port as a gift. If he had noticed Matilda's parcel, he made no mention of it.

He enjoyed the meal for once, finding little fault with the extravagant food and variety of dishes.

'Thank you for my cigars,' he said, his tone condescending. 'They will go well with my port.'

'Do you like the book?' Matilda's voice trembled a little.

Mr Collings pulled the wrapping from the parcel. 'What's this? A novel? You know I don't usually read novels.'

'I'm sorry,' said Matilda. 'The writer is a local man, and his stories are very popular, I believe. I thought it might appeal to you.'

The vicar flicked the pages of *King Solomon's Mines* with a grunt and conceded with, 'Perhaps.'

There was no present for Matilda.

Later that evening, she waited silently in the parlour for the evening tea tray. Her work basket stood open, a piece of charity sewing lay on her lap, and she turned the needle idly between her fingers. Mr Collings had spent the rest of the day in his study, devouring his presents, Matilda assumed. It had grown dark outside, but still their maid had not arrived with the refreshments. The servants would be having their Christmas meal, and Matilda couldn't bear to ring and disturb them. With a sigh, she looked slowly up and out of the window into the garden.

To her horror, she was being watched. Two small children peered at her through the glass. Their faces looked white with cold; their expressions were forlorn. The shock caused Matilda to stab herself with the needle, and with a small cry, she dropped the sewing on the floor. For a moment, she looked in confusion as a drop of blood landed on the baby garment she was making. Then, starting up, she hurried to the window. The faces had gone.

The poor things, she thought. *What can they be doing here? They must be so cold and no doubt hungry too.*

Reaching the window, she looked across the lawn. The two figures were walking towards the churchyard gate.

Matilda dashed out of the room, across the hallway to the front door. As she ran, Mrs Gedge opened the kitchen door carrying the tea tray.

'What on earth is the matter?' Mrs Gedge asked in alarm. She hurriedly put the tray on a side table and followed Matilda.

'There are two children in the garden. Tiny ones, all alone.'

Matilda wrenched open the front door and strode out on the gravel path. Mrs Gedge tried to restrain her. 'Mrs Collings, please don't disturb yourself. I'll get the boy to see them off.'

'No, you don't understand. They've been in the churchyard for days. They may not have a home. I'm so worried about them. Please help me.'

The two women hurried round to the rear of the house, Mrs Gedge trailing behind Matilda as her worry drove her on. She halted momentarily on the lawn, searching this way and that for the children. The gate to the churchyard was swinging open, and Matilda walked quickly on. Mrs Gedge caught up with her before she could go through the gate.

'Mrs Collings,' she said. 'Please stop a moment.'

Matilda swung around. 'We must catch them.'

'No,' said the housekeeper. 'No. That's the last thing we should do.'

'What?'

'Are there two of them?'

'Yes. A boy and a girl.'

'The boy is the elder? They walk holding hands?'

'Yes, exactly that. Do you know them?'

'I think I do,' said Mrs Gedge. She pulled gently at Matilda's arm. 'They are no real children. At least, not any more. No good ever comes of seeing them. Leave them be. Please come back inside.'

'I don't understand,' said Matilda. She was inside the churchyard in a few more paces, but there was no sign of the children. Marching along the path, she searched behind the yew tree and looked up and down the lane without success. The chill air began to make her tremble as she rejoined Mrs Gedge by the wall. 'I think you must explain yourself.'

'If you come inside, then I will.'

As Mrs Gedge settled Matilda back by the parlour fire and brought in the tea tray, she said, 'May I sit a moment?'

'So long as the vicar doesn't join us.'

'Of course.' Mrs Gedge perched on the edge of the vicar's armchair, ready to rise at any moment. 'It's a local story.'

Briefly and with few adornments, the housekeeper told Matilda of the legend of the babes in the wood.

'Do you see them?' Matilda asked.

'No, never.'

'Then why can I? Perhaps my husband is right. Maybe I am mad.'

'Forgive my impertinence, but I do not think so. You still grieve for your babes. I do not believe that grief must pass in a given time, whatever people say.'

'You think because I cannot forget my own children, that I can see these ghostly babes?'

The parlour door opened, and Mrs Gedge was standing by the tray pouring tea before the vicar entered.

'Who is seeing ghosts?' he asked.

'Ghosts, my dear? I merely remembered our lost children.'

'Get out,' he snapped at the housekeeper, who fled. 'You should be over that. It was too many years ago. This melancholia will see you to the asylum if you can't conquer it. Now get to your bed.'

In the silence of her bedroom, Matilda unwrapped her present from Lady Randolph. It was also a story. In fact, it was two books, both volumes of George Elliot's *Middlemarch*. Best of all, inside the front cover of the first was a note.

I am enjoying the blossoming of our new friendship and would like it to continue. As my husband may not stay in Norfolk for long, I would very much like to invite you to visit me in the new year at our home in London. The address is below. Should you ever wish it, a telegram to me will bring a response at any time. Dorothea Randolph.

Chapter Twenty-One

Mr Collings and his wife both rose early on Boxing Day. He strutted around in tweeds, something he rarely had the chance to do, as his position usually dictated more sober dress. Matilda struggled to remember when her husband had last worn this suit, with its grey-green weave flecked with autumnal browns. He had obviously gained weight. She didn't dare to comment. After a hearty breakfast, the vicar fussed in the hallway, trying to make his caped great-coat cover the bulging of his waistcoat buttons.

'Lord Randolph has organised the loan of a shotgun,' he said.

'How kind,' said Matilda with a frown. 'Will you be familiar with it?'

'No matter. The gamekeeper will deal with all that. All I need to do is aim and fire.'

Once Mrs Gedge had managed to fasten the bulging coat, he strode off cheerfully to get into the dog-cart that Lord Randolph had sent to collect him. Matilda sagged with relief at his noisy departure. Now she and Mrs Gedge could begin their own day. As soon as the morning chores had been completed, they set off for Griston Hall.

'This story of the babes is a local legend?' Matilda asked as they walked along the street.

'It's a true story,' replied Mrs Gedge. 'It happened a long time ago, and you know how things grow in the telling.'

'I am sure that I can see them.'

'So others have said. It's the seeing of them that is the warning.'

'Warning?'

'Of something bad that is going to happen soon.'

If Matilda was the only one to see these ghosts, then her husband could be right after all. Her incessant grieving was driving her mad. He had the power to send her to the asylum whenever he pleased, and people rarely returned from such incarcerations.

'Do you mean to an individual?'

'Sometimes.' Mrs Gedge sounded hesitant. 'Other times, it's like a warning of something that will happen to all.'

'Such as? When were they last seen?'

'In 1879,' said Mrs Gedge flatly. 'Just after you arrived here. Mr Wade saw them. He was only a young man then, of course.'

'And did something happen to him?'

'No.'

'Then it's nonsense, surely?'

'Three days after he saw them, smallpox came to the village.'

Matilda halted on the frozen road. Her own children, now lying in the graveyard, had been victims of the same outbreak. She looked at Mrs Gedge, who was blushing to the roots of her hair.

'I'm sorry, Mrs Collings. That's what he claimed. They've not been seen since.'

As Matilda pondered on this unwelcome statement, they heard the clatter of hooves. A procession of carriages and carts bearing the shooting party, the beaters and servants with hampers of food, drove past down the street. She could hear Mr Collings talking loudly. If she had the strength, Matilda would have been embarrassed for him.

At Mrs Gedge's urging, they walked on to the hall. Lady Randolph was waiting for them while her housekeeper arranged the loading of tables with party food suitable for children. They double-checked the parcels and piled a cake and a cheese wheel with each one. They wrapped little presents and buried them in a tub of bran. They washed and loaded apples into a wide, metal washing bucket of clean water with a servant's help. Cushions were brought from various rooms for the children to sit on.

The party was due to start at two, but eager families appeared in the driveway soon after lunchtime. By the appointed hour, there were excited children everywhere, much to Lady Randolph's delight. She clapped her hands and called them to order.

'We'll begin with blind man's bluff,' she announced, producing a scarf.

That was just the start of the chaos. Matilda knew there should be more than forty youngsters there, and trying to stop them from getting over-excited would be impossible. They played hide and seek, and they bobbed for apples. Then they danced as Lady Randolph played the piano for them.

Matilda managed to settle them long enough to play pass-the-slipper before they were led into the dining room and the party feast. The children carried loaded plates to places of safety to eat themselves silly, too busy chewing to make much noise.

Their tummies filled, the children were more amenable to a game of forfeits while they took turns to dig in the bran tub and extract a small present. Although Matilda tried to encourage them to shake the dust off over the tub, the carpet became dusty with bran flakes. Lady Randolph smiled happily.

At four o'clock, the parents began to arrive to collect their youngsters. There was no expectation of further gifts, so the pile of goods, wrapped in their fabric lengths, came as a very welcome surprise. Lady Randolph gave out the bundles, which Mrs Gedge handed to her, and Matilda added the cake and cheese.

'Merry Christmas,' Lady Randolph said to each family. 'And a happy new century in the new year.'

When it was over, Lady Randolph's housekeeper took Mrs Gedge to her private sitting room for a rest while Matilda joined her ladyship in the parlour.

'Did you like your present?'

'Very much,' said Matilda. 'I am sorry I had nothing for you in return.'

'You gave me all this happiness. Will you not call me Dorothea?'

Matilda blushed and nodded. Dorothea patted the sofa, and Matilda sat next to her.

'Did you find my note?'

'Yes.'

'You may contact me at any time. For any reason.'

Matilda looked quizzically at Dorothea, who smiled but offered no further explanation.

'I think the shooting party should return soon. It's getting dark.'

With a jolt, Matilda realised that her friend was right. 'I should go back to the rectory, make sure everything is in order.'

'Do you need Mrs Gedge?'

'Let her rest for a while. I can manage.'

The evening was closing in, and the sky was cloudy. Matilda knew it would be more difficult to see if she didn't hurry. Nonetheless, she paused at her children's grave near the vestry door. Matilda's eyes stung with tears as she dropped to her knees to offer a prayer.

'Did we cause your deaths?' she whispered. 'We should never have come here.'

The ground was still frozen; she could feel it through her skirts. But that didn't account for the sudden chill that ran through her body. Reaching into her coat pocket, she pulled out a spare handkerchief full of sweets, hoping to dry her eyes. Struggling to undo the knot, she pulled off her gloves to wrench at the flimsy fabric, and sugared almonds flew onto the grass of the graves. From the corner of her eye, she saw a tiny hand reach past her to pick one up. A little girl, no more than three years old, stooped beside her, searching through the grass, though her questing fingers could not move the frosted fronds nor pick up an almond when they found one.

The hairs on her skin prickled with fear. Now Matilda was aware of another figure standing on her other side. A boy of five was waiting there, and he held out his hand as if he wanted her to take it. Slowly she opened her palm. The little boy placed his hand in hers. It was tiny, fragile, almost see-through. The skin had no colour, nor did the clothes that covered him. For a moment, she thought the graveyard was visible through him, knowing that must be nonsense. As her fingers closed around his, an icy stab of pain raced through her veins. It spread up her arm and into her heart. Her spine began to lock, and her head began to fall slowly forward. She had no control over herself at all.

Then the sound of racing hooves cut through the night. With a shudder, Matilda's head snapped up to look at the road outside the church. The dog-cart drove frantically towards the rectory. Lord Randolph and one of his guests gripped the side of the cart to prevent themselves from being thrown out. A large bundle lay on the floor. It looked like a man covered in blankets.

Matilda struggled to her feet, bitter with cold. The icy pain had melted from her arm, and the two children had vanished. She staggered towards the rectory garden, where the dog-cart had swung onto the small gravel drive. She could hear shouting, instructions being issued. Their boy servant ran past her at full speed, heading towards the hall. As Matilda crossed the lawn in the dusk, she could see Lord Randolph and the two other men carrying her husband from where he lay in the bottom of the cart into the house.

Now there was chaos of a different kind. Mr Collings was carried to his room, a fire lit, water brought. There was shouting, running for cloths. The guest, mercifully, was a medical man, it was explained. Beyond that, Matilda had no idea what was happening. More people began to arrive.

Mrs Gedge appeared with Lady Randolph, bringing the doctor's bag from the hall. Someone roused Mr Wade at the shop, and treatments were bought. Sitting in a daze, Matilda listened to the voices, the stamping of feet, the groans of her husband. Dorothea sat with her. The parlour fire was lit; a tea tray was brought. Neither of them touched it. Eventually, the noise diminished, and Lord Randolph joined them.

'I am so sorry, my dear,' he began. 'It was an accident. These things sometimes happen when a shooter is less experienced...'

His voice trailed off. Dorothea took Matilda's hand and held it gently.

'The doctor has done his best. Mr Collings has been given morphine for the pain. You can see him now.'

Mrs Gedge was already in attendance when the bewildered Matilda reached her husband's room. The housekeeper guided the stunned woman to a seat by the bed, where her husband lay propped up on pillows. His breathing was ragged, something fluid bubbled in his mouth and his eyes were closed. They had managed to dress him in a nightshirt. Bandages and medical dressings bulked across his chest. Blood seeped through all of it, making a heart-shaped patch that was slowly growing in size.

'The doctor gave him something to make him sleep,' said Mrs Gedge.

'What happened?'

'Gun accident. I don't know how.'

Matilda placed her hands on the bed cover. She saw that one of her fists was balled around a wet handkerchief, the one she had been trying to unknot in the churchyard. She hadn't been aware that she still clutched it.

Mrs Gedge touched her hand lightly while offering a replacement. With infinite slowness, Matilda opened her hand so that the housekeeper could take the dirty item. As her fingers uncurled and the linen slipped away, both women saw the marks. Four tiny lines ran across Matilda's palm. It looked like the imprint of a small child's hand. The marks were red and raw, though the skin was not broken. When Mrs Gedge brought salve, her delicate rubbing shot an icicle up Matilda's arm.

Chapter Twenty-Two

The Reverend Collings never regained consciousness and passed away in the early hours of the 27th of December, which the doctor said was a blessing in disguise, given the serious nature of his injuries. He was buried on New Year's Eve.

Naturally, there was an inquest, during which all the witnesses from the party said the same thing. That Mr Collings had become tired and began to argue with the gunman who assisted him, pulling at the shotgun. Then he'd tripped and fallen onto the barrel as it went off. The conclusion was that it had been an accident, and no one was to blame.

For some days, all that Matilda could think was that she would not need to hide from him or his sly punches and slaps any more. Nor would she ever need to worry again about being sent to the lunatic asylum. Matilda was grateful. Her new friend Dorothea called daily to see how she was, and it was Mrs Gedge who ran the vicarage.

Before long, of course, the bishop in Norwich would need to appoint a replacement. That man would need the vicarage as his home, and Matilda couldn't think what to do. Luckily, Lady Randolph could.

'There is a small cottage near the gates to the hall,' she said. 'You shall move in there. My husband has agreed to a small pension for you. When you feel ready, we shall continue with our school project.'

Mrs Gedge moved into the cottage with Matilda. It was soon a cosy home, full of purpose and busy with projects. The second schoolroom was opened in the autumn. Lady Randolph insisted that they call it the Matilda Collings Room.

When she wasn't staying in London with her friend, Matilda Collings took great delight in guiding the younger pupils in their first educational steps. She and Mrs Gedge also encouraged the older girls to learn other skills that might fit them for work outside the home. In fact, the two became nearly as radical as Lady Randolph, and to the horror of the new vicar, they supported the campaign for votes for women.

Matilda still visited her children's graves regularly, sometimes leaving flowers. She and Mrs Gedge never spoke again of those winter evenings. Nor of the marks in Matilda's hand, which had turned to white scars on the 28th of December and never faded.

1940

These pretty babes went hand-in-hand,
And wander'd up and down;
But never more did see the man,
Approaching from the town.
Their pretty lips with blackberries
Were all besmear'd and dy'd;
And when they saw the darksome night,
They sat them down and cry'd.

Chapter Twenty-Three

❧

Rebecca liked the cut of her WAAF uniform. It not only gave her a sense of authority, but the belt nipped in her waist and showed her figure off nicely. It was similar in colour to the RAF uniform, a particular shade of blue that brought out the cornflower hue of her eyes. Having to share a cramped room with another girl in the accommodation block was a small price to pay for looking so glamorous. She gave herself a satisfied smile in the tiny mirror, smoothed her skirt and headed out to the mess for tea and biscuits. Rebecca wasn't on duty, and with luck, that handsome navigator she liked the look of might be there too. There were few planes available for the mission that evening; several were being repaired. Some of them had a night off.

When war was declared on Germany a year ago, her father had gone berserk. He stamped about the kitchen of their tiny terraced house in Whitechapel, smashing crockery and throwing her mother's precious seaside knick-knacks about the place.

'What did we fight for?' he demanded angrily. 'What was the point? Bloody Huns! Now we'll have to do it all again.'

Finally, he'd headed down to the pub to get drunk with his mates. Many of them had barely survived the last war; they hid their scars, outside and in, without complaint. Rebecca couldn't imagine what it must feel like to face that twice in your life. Not that her father was allowed to join up; he was far too old. Her brother had been conscripted within days; at twenty-one, he was first in line. When he left, her elder sister had arrived to live in the house with her two small children, her husband being away in the merchant navy. It was dreadful. You never knew when someone's temper would explode. The two little ones cried all the time because the tense atmosphere got to them no matter how much comfort was offered by mother, grandmother, or auntie Becca.

She still went to her job as a shop assistant at Harrods, riding the Tube to and from Knightsbridge in her smart store outfit. She still went 'up west' with her friends, eating in the Italian restaurants and catching a film. At least, to begin with, she did. For all the talk of war, nothing seemed to happen before Christmas other than a temporary closure of the cinemas, which only lasted a week and restricted goods for sale in the store. Until they began to round up the families who ran the Italian cafes and send them off to internment camps. Until the recruitment posters crowded out the adverts on the walls of the escalators in the Tube.

January was freezing. Snow fell hard, packing the London pavements with frozen slush that made every activity difficult. The little ones were too small to go out in it, and home became so cold, cramped and damp as to be unbearable to

Rebecca. Her journey to work was regularly disrupted, and the Tube carriages stifled her. There never seemed to be a moment when she wasn't being pushed or crushed. She needed to get away from the racks of damp nappies and grumbling adults. One morning, instead of turning into the staff entrance at the store, Rebecca walked along the Brompton Road until she found a recruiting office and joined the Women's Auxiliary Air Force.

Unsurprisingly, her father threw another temper tantrum when she announced her decision that evening. Rebecca thought that he was worse than the babies sometimes. Her mother looked stunned.

'Where will you go, then?' she asked.

'Don't know,' said Rebecca. 'Some basic training, then a posting. Could be anywhere.'

Anywhere that isn't here, she thought.

Her basic WAAF training at West Drayton revealed a talent for radio operation. The Morse code had remained a mystery for no more than an hour, and map reading was a cinch. Within a few weeks, Rebecca was deemed ready.

'You'll be on an airfield, won't you?' her father said, horrified. 'First places that will be attacked.'

'We all have to do our bit,' she said to him.

His face had creased with anger. 'That's what they said to us. Most of my mates never came back. Can't even leave the women out of it, this time.'

When her posting notification arrived, Rebecca escaped gratefully to Liverpool Street Station at the time stated on her travel permit. Stops at towns and stations broke up the journey, but as all the signs had been taken down, she had no idea where they were heading. They rattled over wide rivers on metal bridges. They were inexplicably turned into sidings to wait for ages until a more important freight train rumbled past. By the time they reached their destination, it was dark outside.

Rebecca joined the other young women in WAAF uniforms, who stood by the ticket barriers, looking around in bewilderment for their transport. Someone should be here to meet them. Eventually, a young RAF officer emerged from the cafe bar, carrying a clipboard and wiping his mouth with the back of his hand. He accounted for each of them in a slurred voice and took them outside to where three small personnel buses waited.

'Welcome to Norwich,' he said. 'Lots of bases around here.'

Squinting at the clipboard, he tried to make out which WAAF should be sent where until one of the girls pulled the list from his hands and read out the orders. Rebecca was horrified to realise that she and one other girl were going with the squiffy officer, and he was driving. There was nothing either of them could do except hang onto the door handles as he occasionally bounced the vehicle off the sides of the minor country road.

It took more than an hour to reach their base. The journey might have been quicker if the officer's driving had been better. Squiffy showed his pass at the gate, and they were let in. He pulled up outside the mess and headed off.

'Where do we report?' Rebecca called after his retreating figure. He turned and shrugged his arms out wide.

'No idea. I'm off to the bar. Welcome anyway. Welcome to Bomber Command in the arse end of nowhere.'

Chapter Twenty-Four

The base was only three years old and was a model of its type. Blenheim bombers stood in hangars with men working on them constantly. Vehicles buzzed between the various buildings, carrying everything from personnel to bombs. It was a real hive of activity, and there was a sense of urgency in everyone's actions and manner.

There were many bases dotted about East Anglia, WAAF Sergeant Susan Hughes explained. RAF Watton was part of Bomber Command, and they were currently very busy. Rebecca was part of an intake of four new women, all destined to help in the ops room. Rebecca and one other would be radio operators; the other two would work as plotters.

'The Spitfire fly-boys in Fighter Command might be getting all the one-to-one action,' Sergeant Hughes said. 'But we are doing our bit to prevent invasion, and it's just as important.'

Regular sorties were being flown by 82 Squadron whenever the weather permitted. Their current main targets were the Nazi landing craft being assembled in occupied Belgium. Each bomber held a three-man crew, and the odds of their survival on any given raid weren't good. Consequently, the men made the most of any free downtime to enjoy themselves.

'While I understand the temptation,' Hughes continued, 'you must be careful of your reputations. The thought that many of our boys may not return will tug at your hearts. Having a drink or a laugh with them is one thing, but I will not tolerate any WAAF caught going further. If I find that you have, you will be sent elsewhere and in disgrace. Have I made myself clear?'

They agreed that she had. It proved harder than Rebecca anticipated. She was gregarious by nature; she enjoyed life and the company. Several of the boys had been quick with their blandishments. She wasn't tempted. Not least because 'boy' was a good term for many of them. Rebecca felt more mature at twenty years old than most of them, though their actual ages might be higher than hers. She felt sorry for them all the same, as the sarge had predicted. She wasn't the one flying over occupied territory in a cramped plane, never knowing if she would survive. The handsome navigator was a different matter. His name was Trevor, and he made her knees go weak. A friendship was developing between them, though she did her best to keep her feelings to herself.

When she entered the mess that afternoon, he was sitting at a table surrounded by half a dozen other men and women. Rebecca collected her teacup, selected two biscuits, and approached the group. Trevor looked up and smiled.

'Budge up,' he said in his broad Yorkshire brogue. 'Let Becca sit here.'

He dragged a chair from the table behind him and pushed it next to his own. With a thrill, Rebecca settled herself in this place of privilege. He was the only one she allowed to called her Becca. The jokes and conversation bounced around them until Trevor leant in close and whispered to her.

'Fancy getting off base tonight? I've got an evening pass. Like to go to the village?'

Rebecca knew that she would. The base was sandwiched between the town of Watton and the village of Griston. There were dances and other entertainments held there in the mess sometimes. Despite that, everyone thought it was more fun to go off base where the higher-ups couldn't monitor their every move.

'I need to ask for permission,' she said.

'Don't be daft.' Trevor winked conspiratorially. 'Old mother hen will say no. They'll never miss you. Charlie's on the gate, and he'll let us back in.'

It took a little more persuasion before Rebecca agreed. Later that evening, the pair skirted the rear of the accommodation blocks and climbed into a transport bus that Trevor had, somehow, obtained the keys for and headed out. He chose to go to Griston, to Rebecca's disappointment. She had been there long enough to know that a pub in Watton would be livelier. Parking outside the Waggon and Horses, Trevor lead her into the snug. It was crowded and smoky.

An old boy obliged them by making room at his table. Trevor went to buy their drinks while Rebecca looked around the room. The customers were mostly older men who looked like farmworkers. Their mood was sombre. Since Dunkirk, everyone knew that the war wasn't going well, whatever the official line might be.

'Why did you want to come here?' Rebecca asked when Trevor returned.

'Reminds me of home,' he said. 'My granny brought me up. Runs a pub called the Spread Eagle in a village called Wragby. Haven't been back for months now. Went straight from training to squadron.'

They were just settling in to their first drink when the bar door crashed open and a village bobby staggered in, panting as if he had cycled at full speed.

'Get that door shut,' called the landlady. A customer obliged, while the bobby bent double, clutching his chest. 'Whatever is the matter, Geoff?'

'I seed 'em,' the man stammered. He pulled off his helmet, plonked it down, and leant heavily on the table.

'Who? What?' demanded voices from the crowd. Trevor rose from his seat.

'You mean Nazis? Have they invaded?'

Geoff shook his head; his breathing was easing. Wide-eyed, he looked around the room. 'No, not the Germans. It's worser 'an that. I saw 'em.'

He emphasised 'them' as if he had seen some kind of monster. 'The children. Walking hand in hand down the road out yonder. Heading for your lot.'

He pointed at their uniforms. Someone at the back of the room laughed. Others joined in, but not everyone. A few shared hurried glances with worried eyes.

'Oh, give it over,' said one customer. 'No such thing as ghosts. Just a story, thas all. Have a drink to calm your nerves, bor.'

'Reckon, you've had too many already,' said the landlady, to general amusement. She pulled him a pint anyway.

'I tell you, I seed 'em,' said Geoff.

'In this dark?'

'I props up me bike on the bank and follows them. Into the woods they went, and I went too, 'til there was so many trees I could hardly see for them. I kept calling to them, but they didn't look round. Walked right through and out the other side, opposite the base. By the time I got there, they'd vanished. God help them who is out there flying tonight. It's going to happen again.'

If Geoff had been expecting a reaction, the silence that fell around him probably wasn't the one he would have imagined. Rebecca saw that almost every drinker had turned to look at Trevor and herself.

'Come on, Geoff,' said the landlady. 'You should be supporting our boys, not frightening them. Drink up.'

It was enough to break the silence, but the atmosphere remained glum. Hardly the evening out she had been hoping for. When Trevor went to get another round, Rebecca turned to the old boy sitting with them.

'What did he mean? What children?'

'You don't know where you are then?'

'Norfolk.'

'Did you like fairy tales when you were a young 'un?'

'Sort of.'

'The babes in the wood?' the old boy asked quietly. 'Abandoned in the woods by their wicked uncle?'

'I saw that in a pantomime once,' Rebecca said. The memory of a happier time made her smile.

'Well, it was those woods,' he said, pointing over his

shoulder. 'Wayland Woods. You can see it from the base. The house the villain wanted to steal was Griston Hall. You can see that from the base too.'

'So, these children he thinks he's seen, they're ghosts?'

'In the old story, the children died in the woods and were supposed to be covered in leaves by birds to bury them. People here claim they see them sometimes. It's never a good sign. A bad omen, they say. Someone is going to die.'

'People die all the time in war,' said Rebecca quietly.

'That they do.'

'What did he mean by it happening again?'

The old boy pointed in the vague direction of the base. 'The men up there have had it tough. Ask your mates. But it might be something more personal, like.'

'Do locals see them all the time then?'

'Not been seen for years. Until that place was finished.'

'The base?'

'And seeing them brings on a tragedy, always.'

Chapter Twenty-Five

Charlie let them back in without a fuss. The mission for that evening was already completed. The bombers were straggling back to the base. Rebecca automatically began to count for losses. By some miracle, there were none. If this fairy tale about the children was true, then it hadn't been a warning about tonight's raid.

Over breakfast, Rebecca asked Sergeant Hughes about the squadron's bad luck.

'We don't talk about it much,' she said. 'Though it's no secret. The squadron is lucky to still be here at all.'

'Why?'

'You can see that we are under capacity?'

'Isn't that why we're due three new bombers?'

'It is. You see, we have lost our entire complement of planes and their crews. Twice.'

'Twice?'

Heads turned sharply towards them; the mess fell silent.

Rebecca looked down at her bowl and waited until the conversation started again.

'Once in May and again in August,' said Hughes. 'Each time, a single plane returned. The rest shot down over occupied territory, most of their crews dead or captured. Or at least we hope so. A couple of them even managed to get back to us from Dunkirk.'

Rebecca thought about the old boy's words. These must be the tragedies he meant.

'They tried to shut the squadron down,' continued Hughes. 'Only the intervention of the C.O. prevented us from being dispersed to other parts of the Command. Our survival is much in doubt.'

Rebecca was proud to see the bombers arrive in convoy as she headed to the ops room to work. She watched as the men gathered around the new planes, talking with the Air Transport Auxiliary female pilots almost as equals, before taking them to the mess to celebrate. The forecast was good for the evening, and a big raid was planned. They were doing short shifts with long breaks during the day; everyone would be working tonight.

It was almost her meal break when Rebecca began to pick up chatter from other bases. Turning to her partner, she held up her hands as a question. The other girl shrugged and frowned.

'What's happening in Essex?' Rebecca asked, pulling off her headset. 'What do they mean.'

'Not sure. North Kent are getting hysterical by the sound of it. Wait a mo.'

They both checked again, spoke to their counterparts on other bases, not quite able to believe what they were hearing.

'I'm going to fetch the C.O.,' said the other girl. She dropped her headset and ran out of the radio station. Rebecca retuned and picked up her contact at RAF Bradwell Bay.

'Can you confirm the sightings?'

'Spotters say there are dozens of them,' said the Bradwell girl. 'Converging on the Thames and heading towards London.'

'In broad daylight?' Rebecca could barely believe it.

'Yes. We've had reports from the barrage and anti-aircraft posts. Estimated up to one hundred Luftwaffe bombers have entered British airspace in several waves. The first group is about ten minutes away from central London on their current course.'

Rebecca scribbled the details on her notepad, repeating them back to Bradwell for verification. Even as she signed off, the C.O. was leaning over her shoulder to pick up the pad.

'Is this confirmed?'

'As much as it can be, sir,' she said.

'They'll be heading for the docks and railway yards,' he said. 'God help anyone who lives near them. Thank you, ladies.'

When her relief arrived, Rebecca headed to the mess for her evening meal. Trevor was already there, leaning on the bar with several others listening intently to the radio. Their bodies masked the details of the broadcast, although the BBC announcer's voice sounded high pitched and stressed.

'What's happened? What's going on?'

Trevor's pilot glanced at her. 'German planes. Waves of them. They are bypassing our defences and getting to

London. They've bombed the place. No one has ever seen anything like it before. There are fires everywhere.'

'All of it?' Rebecca gasped.

'The docks and the East End have been targeted most. They say it's like an inferno, absolute hell.'

She staggered with shock, grabbing at Trevor's arm for support. 'My family. They live in Whitechapel.'

The pilot looked at her with sympathy. 'Bad luck. That's been badly hit.'

She ran back to the ops room. Sergeant Hughes was already there, getting ready for that evening's raid. The sarge's face was pale, and her jaw firmly clenched so that she wouldn't betray her emotions.

'What's the latest?' she asked. When Rebecca told her about the broadcast, she added, 'the damn nerve of these Nazis.'

'I need to contact my family. They may have been bombed.'

Hughes wrote out a chitty and handed it to her. 'You may send a telegram. Here's the authorisation.'

Rebecca dashed across to the comms office, grabbed a slip, addressed it and wrote:

ARE YOU SAFE SEND NEWS OF ALL FAMILY STOP NO MATTER WHAT STOP

She handed it over to the WAAF behind the desk, who read it and gave Rebecca a look of sympathy. 'Ops room for any reply?'

'Yes. All night.'

'You realise it's chaos down there? There may be no one free to deliver this.'

'My mum and dad, my sister, and her two kids. They thought I would be the one in danger.'

'I'll do my best.'

There was nothing else Rebecca could do. Returning to the mess, she collected her meal. It tasted like sawdust to her, and after pushing it around the plate for several minutes, she abandoned it. Trevor brought two cups of tea and sat down next to her without speaking. He put one cup in front of her, then placed his hand over hers, and they waited. It was the 7th of September.

Chapter Twenty-Six

There was no reply from her family by the time Rebecca returned to the ops room. The planes took off in small groups, with a WAAF radio operator monitoring each bomber's progress. Their positions were tracked on a map table in the centre of the room; their flight path indicated either Belgium or Holland. Headphones clamped to her ears, Rebecca listened for the voices of the crew amongst the whines and hiss that plagued the frequencies. It didn't take long for the pilots to report that they were flying through German flak. The terrible losses of the summer were still preying on her mind, and Rebecca offered a silent prayer for Trevor's safety. All the operators knew they could be the last ones to hear these brave men alive.

The squadron had been airborne for more than an hour when a WAAF from comms arrived with a reply from Rebecca's family.

ALL SAFE STOP EVERYWHERE ON FIRE STOP NEED TO EVACUATE CHILDREN STOP DAD

Sergeant Hughes came over, and Rebecca showed her the message.

'Short tea break on a rota,' she said. The trolley stood in the corner. 'You first.'

Rebecca took her cup outside, leaning thankfully against the tower wall. She was so relieved. Her father was right. Her sister, with two youngsters, should have agreed to the evacuation before now. They had all tried to persuade her, but she'd refused.

'Good news?'

Rebecca started. She hadn't heard the group captain walk out to join her. He was an older, senior officer, and she would not have expected him to be interested in her. She snapped up to attention.

'Relax. Sergeant Hughes told me about your family. They've had it bad in London.'

'Yes, sir. They're all safe, though.'

'Good stuff.' He lit a cigarette and drew deeply onto it, and the end glowed in the darkness.

'I wish my sister would evacuate.'

'She younger than you?'

'No, sir. But she has two children under five.'

'Lots of vaccees up here. She should ask.'

'Yes, sir.' Rebecca turned her gaze across the grass runway to the far perimeter fence. To her surprise, she could see something small and bright, glimmering steadily. 'Sir? Can you see that? Is it a torch?'

'It shouldn't be. No one is allowed over there.' He walked back into the ops room, returning swiftly with a pair of binoculars. 'Where?'

Rebecca pointed. 'It's only small.'

'Can't see it,' he said. 'I'll take your word for it all the same. Can't be too careful. Here, you try.'

He handed over the binoculars and went back to the ops room. She lifted the heavy glasses and tried to find the light, scanning to the left and right until something flickered into her line of sight. Rebecca focused on the bright spot.

It wasn't a torch or a car headlight, as she had been expecting. Her heart began to pound because she didn't believe what she was looking at.

Outside the high metal wire fence stood two children. They were holding hands, and unmoving, they gazed into the airfield. They didn't look any older than her sister's kids. They couldn't possibly be alone. She scanned a little to either side without finding any trace of an adult. They seemed oddly visible, as though someone was shining a light onto them and illuminating their clothes. Like that game children sometimes played of shining a torch under their chins in the dark to make themselves look monstrous.

Somewhere near the guard post, Rebecca heard a vehicle fire up. The captain returned.

'Found it?'

'Yes, sir,' she said, hesitating to say what she thought she saw. She pointed along the fence. 'Over near the woods.'

'Just sent a couple of men over to have a look.'

'Might just be kids, mucking about. With a torch or something.'

'Then they'll be seen off. Can't be having that.' He took the binoculars back and scanned for himself. 'Nope, still can't see it. You've got very good eyesight. Watch and tell me when the men get there.'

Rebecca refocused in the same place. The two children

now seemed to be standing inside the fence. She knew that wasn't possible. It was well maintained, there was no gate in that section, and patrols constantly inspected the perimeter.

As she watched, the little boy saw her. His eyes locked onto hers, and he raised his arm to point straight at her. Her skin grew clammy; her breath began to shorten.

'You all right?' The captain's voice jolted her. She glanced at him and nodded.

When Rebecca looked again, the children were even closer. Now they stood on the grass next to the landing area. They couldn't have run that far that quickly. His hand still pointing at her, the boy pulled his little sister gently along. Somehow, they were covering huge amounts of distance with each toddling step. It was impossible. His eyes never lost focus on Rebecca. Closer and closer they came, holding her mesmerised. She began to shake and sweat, unable to tear her gaze away. Surely the captain could see them now?

'Sir,' she said urgently. 'It's two children. They've got into the base.'

'They can't have,' he snapped.

'But I can see them. On the runway. I don't understand. I can't...'

She dropped the binoculars with a cry as the children seemed to be swelling up to fill her entire view. 'Two children. Holding hands.'

'Dear God,' said the group captain. 'Not again.'

Chapter Twenty-Seven

Trevor was lucky. They lost two planes that night, but his wasn't one of them. Rebecca was too busy at her station to think about what she had seen or the group captain's response. Afterwards she was so tired, it took the last of her energy to stagger back to bed and fall asleep in her uniform. Another mission was planned for the next night, and after just six hours of sleep, Rebecca was roused by her roommate.

'If you hurry, you have time to wash and change,' she said. 'I'm done already.'

When they reached the mess, a group of personnel was standing around the radio, listening in silence. The news from London was grim. Whole streets flattened; churches damaged; factories and docks still burning. The bombing had continued wave after wave through the night until the small hours.

'They're calling it a Blitz,' said Trevor when he joined her at the table. 'Like Blitzkrieg, you know.'

'I don't know what to do about my family.' Rebecca tried hard to eat her single rasher of bacon.

'You can't make them do anything,' reasoned Trevor. 'They have to want to move. It might not happen again, anyway.'

Trevor couldn't have been more wrong. The bombing was a change of Nazi policy. The RAF had upset their plans for invasion, and now they were out to subdue the people by bombing them out of work, food and home.

The skies were clear that evening, and the bombers left in formation to somewhere over the near continent. It meant that the German planes were able to come the other way to bomb London again.

'The worst is the incendiaries,' said Sergeant Hughes. 'They not only set the place on fire; they also act as a beacon so they can fly at night as well.'

Despite her worries about her family, Rebecca had to get on with her job. There was no sympathetic tea break that night, nor on the following two nights. Her position was no different from many others by then. The Blitz on London continued, though the planes came exclusively at night now, as the anti-aircraft stations began to pick off those who dared to try in the daylight. Trevor's luck was holding, though even he couldn't say why. Nor had she seen the strange children or heard anyone else mention them since that night.

'I've got an idea,' Trevor said one morning as they sat together at breakfast. 'My gran is getting on a bit, and they could do with some help in the Spread Eagle. Do you think your family might like to move up there?'

'Would it be any better?' Rebecca asked. She knew that

Trevor's home was in the West Yorkshire coalfields. Nearby cities were likely to be targets too. 'I mean any safer?'

'I reckon it would. The village is quiet enough, and Wakefield is at least ten miles away. I sent Gran a letter a few days ago. She says that they can try. There would be room for your parents and your sister with her children. They're short of staff at the big house too.'

Trevor handed over the letter. It was addressed in a spidery, old-fashioned script. The invitation was clear, and for the first time in days, Rebecca smiled.

'Thank you so much,' she said. 'I'll write as soon as I've finished my breakfast.'

The letter was soon scribbled and delivered to the comms office.

The weather grew cloudy and for two nights the squadron was grounded. On the third day the skies cleared and another night's raid was scheduled. For a while, Rebecca sat with Trevor on a bench near the mess, enjoying the warmth of the sun. They had fallen into being together, like some old married couple at ease with each other. As the evenings drew in, they would share a kiss before Trevor went to suit up. He never asked her for more, and she was grateful for his respect. The danger he was in seemed to both accelerate and dampen their feelings. They had become a couple in such a short time, but they never shared those words that would make it somehow official. As if it would be a jinx and, once spoken, it couldn't be retracted.

So, neither said, 'I love you.' If Sergeant Hughes was concerned, she never mentioned it.

'Long one tonight,' said Trevor when they parted. That meant it would be even more dangerous. More chances that they would be shot down, and almost certainly that they were going to a more heavily defended target.

Rebecca wasn't allowed to monitor Trevor's plane. Perhaps that was a quiet acknowledgement of their burgeoning relationship. It turned out to be a good thing. The mission took them to Denmark. One plane was lost to a flak battery on the coast, another on the approach to the target. One by one, they dropped their loads. Sweeping back out over the North Sea, the remaining planes began to head home, Trevor's at the rear. Their radio operator lost contact as they passed the island of Romo.

At first, Rebecca was too busy with her own pilot to realise. Until it was her turn to have a tea break. Sergeant Hughes tapped her on the shoulder and took over her station. As she collected her cup, she realised that the other WAAF was staring at her anxiously and biting at her lower lip. Knowing better than to make a scene, Rebecca headed outside into the cooler night air.

As she waited, desperate to know what was happening, she grew colder and colder. Shuffling from foot to foot to keep warm, Rebecca wished she had put more sugar in her tea. That was supposed to give you energy, wasn't it? The other WAAF joined her, cup in hand.

'Trevor is your boyfriend, isn't he?' she asked. Rebecca froze. The woman continued in a low voice, 'They've been hit. As far as I can tell, the fire is out. The plane is damaged, limping home. I'm sorry.'

'Thank you.' They both knew that she shouldn't be sharing this information.

With a nod, the other woman began to walk around the tower to stretch her legs. Rebecca watched her go, tipped the last cold dregs of her tea onto the grass and turned to go back to her station. Maybe it was her heightened state of worry, perhaps it was too many late nights, but she felt that she was being watched.

Watched by two children who stood on the far side of the runway. Glittering white and holding hands. The boy raised his arm and pointed to her. Rebecca screamed and dropped her teacup onto the floor. It smashed.

Chapter Twenty-Eight

❧

Rebecca remained in the ops room as each of the Blenheims returned, waiting for Trevor. Finally, his plane began its descent, and she stood outside in the dark. The engine's sound reached her first, gathering in volume until she could just make out the weaving wings. As the wheels in the undercarriage hit the grass, the engine seemed to cut out, and the plane hurtled past as it struggled to brake in time. It was a close-run thing. The plane juddered to a halt with its nose only yards away from the perimeter fence.

In the light from the cockpit, she saw the pilot and gunner climb out. Trevor didn't. Rebecca ran towards the plane as the ground crew rushed past in a vehicle, followed by an ambulance. By the time she reached the scene, Trevor was lying on the grass, the legs of his trousers burnt away and bloody, his hands covered in burns and oily dirt. The ambulance crew lifted him gently onto a stretcher, loaded him into the ambulance and drove away. She stood silently while the men swirled past her, shouting about the flight and the condition of the plane, until the pilot took pity on her.

'He's in the best place,' he said. 'The M.O. will take care of him.'

'What happened?'

'Took a spot of flak on his side.' He pointed to the damage on the aircraft. 'Luckily, it only clipped us. Trev got the fire out before it did too much damage. Burnt his hands, and it caught on his trousers too. You should go back now.'

Walking back towards her accommodation, Rebecca felt as if she was being watched again. When she looked back at the plane, beyond the fence, she was almost unsurprised to see the two ghostly children. With a shiver, she headed for her bed. It was tiredness and stress, that was all. She was hallucinating. There were no such things as ghosts.

The next morning, Rebecca was allowed to visit Trevor on the hospital ward. He seemed pleased to see her, although he looked sleepy. His hands were both bandaged, and a metal frame raised the bedclothes above his legs. They had propped him up with pillows.

'Never try to put out a fire with your bare hands,' he said.

'Brave thing to do,' she said. 'I think you saved everyone.'

He looked embarrassed. 'They would have done the same for me.'

'What does the doctor say?'

'I'm going to be out of action for some time. My hands are worse than my legs. Trousers caught on fire, you know?'

She knew. 'You're here; that's the main thing.'

'Not for long,' he said. 'Sending me home to get well. Back to the Spread Eagle and my gran. Did your family get in touch?'

Rebecca waved a letter. 'Came this morning. They've written to your gran, and then we'll see. London is getting bombed every night now. Nowhere is spared.'

'I'll be there on sick leave for a while. I can help settle them in. I won't be much use to Gran like this.'

'Mum says that they have persuaded Dot to take the kids abroad. So it would just be my mum and dad.'

'Dot?'

'My sister and her two little ones. Don't know how they did it, but the three of them are off to Canada.'

'How?' Trevor was beginning to drift to sleep. Rebecca checked the letter.

'Mum says, "Dad managed to secure passage for all three on the *City of Benares*. Leaves Liverpool in a few days, and we are packing up while Dot tries to get train tickets." Bless them.'

'Sounds great.' Trevor's eyes closed, and his voice petered out. She left him to rest.

During the afternoon, Rebecca and three of the other girls were passed out to go into Watton for a couple of hours. There were local shops to visit and a pleasant little tea room where they could have a break from the stress of their work. Rebecca headed to a shop where she had her eye on a pretty blouse in the window. Pondering on taking a risk and learning to knit a cardigan to go with it, she was surprised when an older man stopped next to her. He leant on his walking stick, looked in the window, then at her, and smiled.

'You doing all right?'

It was the old boy from the Waggon and Horses. The one who had told her about the ghostly children.

'I'm well, thank you.'

'That's a pretty colour,' he said, pointing to some wool in the display. 'If you get time to knit, that is.'

'Sometimes,' she replied. 'How are you?'

'All right, I suppose. Seen any ghosts lately?' He laughed quietly.

'As a matter of fact, I have. Do you know much about these children?'

'I was joking.' He looked at her in surprise.

'I know. I'm not.'

'You see them? Where?'

'Near the base, around the fence sometimes. They frighten me.'

'Ah, that they should. Never a good thing.'

'Have they been seen a lot recently?' Rebecca persisted.

'People say so.'

'When?'

He looked back at the wool in the window. 'That colour would suit you.'

'When?' Rebecca asked again, more forcefully this time. 'I mean, I get it that they are a bad omen and all that.'

'Once in May,' he said quietly. 'Again, in August.'

Rebecca thought about this. The old boy turned and took a couple of steps away from her. She put her hand gently on his sleeve. 'Just before the two raids? When the squadron was wiped out?'

'Both times,' he said. 'If you be seeing them again now, it's going to get bad again.'

'Then why does the boy point at me?'

'What?' He looked up. 'Never heard o' that before.'

'I feel like they're chasing me. None of it can be real, can it? I'm just tired, and my imagination is running riot.'

'If you say so.'

'What would you say?'

'P'rhaps it's not the crews that's facing trouble. Maybe it's you.'

'More likely, my family,' she said. 'They are getting bombed every night.'

'Well, that might be so. Think on it. The babes are a warning. You should take notice if you think it be for yourself. Good luck, miss.'

He shuffled away. Rebecca watched him go until he reached the butcher's shop and turned in.

He's just winding me up, the old goat, she thought and gave herself an impatient shake. Then she went into the drapers' shop to buy the pretty wool and a pattern.

Chapter Twenty-Nine

The mission that night was stood down before teatime. Rebecca hurriedly ate her meal, then went to the medical ward to help Trevor with his. He could just about hold a fork to pick up the food, but cutting it up was beyond his injured hands. He seemed more cheerful than earlier that day.

'Transport has been arranged; heading off in the morning to get the train.'

'Can you manage that on your own?'

'No choice, have I?' Trevor glanced at her, then concentrated on picking up another mouthful of food. 'I'll miss you.'

'And I'll miss you,' she said. 'You'll be back when you're better.'

'Could get posted to another squadron. Might not be fit to fly again either. Depends on these damn burns.'

'It will all work out fine,' she said and prayed that it would.

'You due any leave soon?'

'Don't know. I hope so.'

'You could come up to the pub as well. Meet everyone, see how your folks are doing.'

As these things weren't settled yet, all Rebecca could do was smile, agree and hope. That's all any of them could do.

It turned out that her roommate was a demon knitter. That evening, she gave Rebecca her first lesson. Despite finding it a challenge, it felt calming to be concentrating on something other than dials or the sound of radio static and chatter in her headphones. When they settled down to sleep, the base outside was still working. They were all used to it now, and she soon fell asleep.

The place had grown silent when Rebecca heard a tapping at the window in the middle of the night. A tiny, insistent, rhythmical tapping. With a yawn, she rolled out of bed and smiled despite the cold floor under her feet. She lifted the blackout curtain at the corner to peek out, half-expecting it to be Trevor on his way to his transport. The smile froze on her lips.

A tiny grey hand was reaching up from under the outside windowsill, index finger tapping, tapping, scratching, tapping. Startled, Rebecca stepped back, only to feel herself falling, dizzy and bewildered. She expected to hit the floor any moment, now or now, or even now. She was falling through a blackness so absolute that she couldn't find a single object for her brain to seize on to help it make sense of the void.

With a thump, Rebecca landed on her hands and knees on the grass outside the accommodation block. Blood seeped from grazes, and she shook her head to clear it. Now a small, gleaming hand reached under her dangling hair to touch her arm. The fingers wrapped themselves around her wrist, the touch so cold it burnt like a branding iron. Her locked muscles refused to move as, with a gasp, she tried to pull away. All she could do was raise her head.

The boy was looking straight into her eyes, his face too solemn for such a small child. Over his shoulder, Rebecca could see the little girl. She wanted to cry out, shake off his hand, run away. It must be a nightmare. A voice in the back of her brain tried to shout. *Wake up.* She couldn't.

The tiny hand released its grip, and she lurched forward onto the grass. It knocked the wind out of her lungs, which no amount of effort could replace. *This is what it is like to drown,* her brain screamed. *Breathe.* With a supreme effort, air rushed into her body, making her cough and splutter. Rolling over, she tried to stand. The two children had retreated to the end of the hut. Their backs were turned; they were walking away. She scrambled after them.

'What do you want?' Rebecca gasped. 'Why me? I don't even believe in bloody ghosts.'

Across the grass they drifted, Rebecca stumbling after them, always lagging. Now they were not alone. More ghostly figures drifted out of reach: a woman, with two other children walking beside her, their backs turned. Rebecca realised with horror that she knew them. It was Dot, with her two noisy, energetic kids. Her niece and nephew.

'Dot,' she called. 'Stop. Wait.'

The three turned to face her. Each looked impassively on as Rebecca tried to reach them. With a sudden shock, she realised they were dripping wet. Her hands stretched out to touch them.

'Rebecca,' said a voice sharply. 'Wake up.'

Now she was lying on the floor of her bedroom, legs tangled in sheets and blankets. For some reason, her face was wet. Could it be tears? She rubbed away the damp. Her roommate was shaking her shoulder with one hand and held a cup in the other.

'Sorry about that. You were having a bad nightmare. I couldn't wake you, no matter how hard I shook you. I had to throw some water on your face.'

Trembling with exhaustion, Rebecca levered herself up onto her bed.

'You going to be all right?'

'Yeah.'

Settling back onto her pillows, she looked at her wrist. A set of three tiny striped welts stood proud of her pale skin. It hurt to touch them. When she tried to sleep, the nightmare still played behind her eyelids, as if she were watching a film. Why were they all so wet?

Then understanding dawned. The evacuee boat, the *City of Benares*. Perhaps it was because her family were so much in her mind, but Rebecca was suddenly certain she knew what the ghostly children were trying to tell her. If Dot and her kids got on that boat, then they would be drowned.

Chapter Thirty

Rebecca was jolted awake by the sound of tapping on the window. Her heart in her mouth she pulled up the corner of the curtain, and was relieved to see Trevor stood outside, leaning on a crutch. She threw on her dressing gown and dashed out. It was early, and the base was coming back to life in the morning sun.

'Just off for the train,' he said. 'They're taking me to Thetford on the bus.'

'Can you take something for me?' she asked. 'In case my family are with your gran?'

'Sure. I'll walk slowly. My legs are still sore anyway.'

She hurried back inside and pulled out her writing paper to scribble a hasty note urging her mum to prevent Dot and the children from going for the boat. Stuffing it inside an envelope, she raced across the grass to catch up with Trevor.

'Here.' Rebecca pushed the envelope into his jacket pocket. 'You won't forget, will you? It's really urgent.'

'I won't forget,' he said. With a smile, he leant down and

kissed her. The bus driver gave them a wolf whistle, then yelled at Trevor to get a move on. 'You should write home as well if it's that urgent.'

'I know.' She helped him up the stairs onto the bus. 'Safe journey.'

Hurrying back to her room, Rebecca dressed quickly and sat on her bed to write another letter to her parents at home. Now that she was thinking about what to say, it seemed that words deserted her. How could she demand that Dot and the children stay behind if they had the chance of a new life in a country that was unlikely to be bombed like London? It sounded wild and strange to say that two ghostly children had warned her. Her family were neither religious nor superstitious. They'd think she had gone doolally tap. Even so, she wrote on. She called it a premonition and then backed it up by saying they knew something on the base that she couldn't explain. This last was an outright lie, but she didn't care.

She dropped the letter off at the comms room, then headed to the mess for breakfast. It was still early, so the place was half-empty. Tired and over-wrought, tears welled up in her eyes as she stared at her egg and toast. It wasn't until Sergeant Hughes sat opposite her that Rebecca pulled a handkerchief from her pocket and blew her nose.

'Is it serious between you two?' the sergeant asked.

'Oh. I think so. I don't know.'

'Why are you upset then?'

'Worried about my family. Stuck in London.'

'The Blitz is terrible, though somehow people seem to be adapting and looking after each other.'

'Yes, ma'am.'

Sergeant Hughes made short work of her breakfast.

'Things are looking bad at the moment. We're on standby all the time. It would be difficult to be short an operator. More tea?'

Rebecca wondered if she was trying to explain something to her or just talking out loud to sort out her thoughts. The sergeant returned with two cups.

'Would it help if you had a very short pass?'

'Oh yes, Sarge. It would help ever so much. They have an offer to get out of the city. Perhaps I could persuade them to take it.'

'I'll see what I can do. You're not the only one, you know.'

'Yes, ma'am. I know.'

The day dragged. The order came to be ready for another night flight, and the base busied itself. The second order in mid-afternoon stood them down. The bomb loading crew began to unload the planes again; they couldn't be left standing with all that explosive in them. A third order put them back on standby, and exhaustedly, they prepared the planes for a second time and the crews reported for orders. It was almost a full moon. A bombers' moon, as they had all come to call it. Eleven Blenheims set off just before midnight.

The raid was short. The Netherlands was the closest point in Europe to Norfolk. The flying time was under an hour. Their target was heavily defended, and no one could report whether they had achieved any damage to the new German installation on the Dutch coast. The radio operators pulled off their headsets one by one as three more planes went down, with the loss of all on board. They counted the eight lucky ones back onto the ground.

Rebecca crossed to the mess with the other WAAFs to get

a bedtime cocoa. She looked along the perimeter fence. There was no sign of ghostly children or hovering white lights. It had all been just a nightmare. Maybe she'd been ill with worry about Trevor, and now he was off home. It was an awful thing to think, she knew, but at least it kept him out of danger for a few weeks. If only her family would leave London to stay safe, then she could get on with her job.

Chapter Thirty-One

They only had five hours of sleep, but that was the same as the men. Rebecca and her roommate were back at a WAAF briefing immediately after breakfast. More advanced radios were being supplied shortly, and training sessions were being held. For now, all they had were diagrams, which they poured over as best they could for the rest of the day. She found it hard to concentrate. The squadron was put on standby again, despite their depleted stock of planes. They stopped to grab a quick meal before the operation began. Sergeant Hughes told Rebecca to stay behind.

'You are the lucky one,' she said and handed over a pass and a travel warrant. 'Forty-eight hours. If you go now, you can ask transport to take you to the railway station before the last London train. Be back on time, or I'll put you on a charge.'

Rebecca ran back to her room, threw a few clothes in her holdall and raced to the mess. Spotting one of the drivers finishing his meal, she begged a lift, and reluctantly he agreed. He went to sign out of camp while she threw a sausage between two slices of bread to eat on the train. In minutes they were trundling towards Thetford.

It was dusk, and as they drove through the woods to reach the main road, the driver put on his headlights. The covers created two narrow bars of light on the road, which were just enough to see by but intended to disguise the vehicle's presence. Rebecca watched as rabbits ran out of their way, scuts flashing white in the gloom. As they headed out of the woods, a flash of white to her left amongst the trees made Rebecca's head jerk to the look out of the side window.

Was that the ghostly children? She tried to pinpoint the light as they left the trees.

'I'm going. I'm doing my best,' she murmured.

'Say what?' asked the driver.

'Nothing, I'm just worried about my family, that's all.'

'London?'

'Whitechapel.'

'Ah. Got you.'

They didn't speak again until he dropped her at the railway station in Thetford. Then he wished her good luck. 'Hope they're all right.'

The London train was late. Rebecca had eaten her hasty sandwich, then a slice of stale cake with a cup of tea, which she bought in the station buffet. When the train did arrive, it was half-empty, and she soon found a vacant carriage. No one disturbed her or even joined her as they headed south. It seemed an interminable journey. When they reached the outskirts of the city, the skyline glowed red.

They could go no further than Stratford. That evening's

raid had already begun. The Underground had stopped running. The guard told her that many of the stations were being co-opted as air-raid shelters. Outside she managed to find a bus that took her as far as it could.

'You'd best get underground,' the conductor advised her. 'It's really bad tonight.'

She began to walk. All around her, she heard the thud of bombs dropping. The docks were the target again; the glow of fires looked to be coming mostly from that direction. The streets were devastated, buildings demolished, homes wrecked, shops in tatters. The Mile End Road was the most direct route, though most buildings were now just piles of debris. Rebecca made slow progress. Planes droned overhead. There was the whistle of a bomb falling, followed by its explosion. Shaken by the noise and the crashes that followed, she hurried on. The conductor had been right; she needed to get out of this. It was pointless trying to find anyone until the all-clear had sounded. The entrance to Whitechapel Tube Station finally reared up in the light from the burning buildings, and she descended gladly.

The platforms were open to the sky, as they often were on this line, which had been one of the earliest to be built. The stairwell was crowded with people. Rebecca stepped carefully around them until she reached the bottom. There were lights on in the tunnels. More people were sitting carefully on either side of the tracks, their backs against the brick walls.

'It's all right,' said a woman who sat on the bottom step. 'They turn the tracks off during raids; just be careful.'

Rebecca headed into the tunnel. It was filthy with soot. Mice and rats scurried along underneath the central electric rail, going about their underground lives just as they always did. Stepping firmly onto each track sleeper, she managed to get some way inside when a huge explosion made the whole place shake. The noise was deafening. Dust blasted down the tunnel on a storm of heated air. Children cried. People screamed. The lights flickered, went out, and thankfully came back on. Some people began to stand up and move further down the tunnel, presumably hoping it would offer more protection. There was remarkably little conversation. She blinked the dust from her eyes.

'Becca? Is that really you?'

Shaking the dust from her hands, Rebecca wiped her face and looked around the cloudy tunnel.

'Is that really you?'

Now she recognised the voices. It was her mum and dad. Scanning the sheltering people, she finally spotted them. Her mother had risen in disbelief. Rebecca moved as quickly as she could, past the recumbent figures and around those who were moving. She found herself being hugged and smothered in kisses with a cry of joy and a sob from her mother.

'What are you doing here?'

'Looking for you,' said Rebecca. She transferred her hugs to her father, who grunted with pleasure. 'Where's Dot? Did you get my letter?'

'What letter? We haven't managed to get home for a couple of days.'

'Has she gone to Liverpool? She can't get on that boat.'

'What on earth do you mean? It's best for them all to get away.'

'Something terrible will happen if they leave. We have to stop them.'

'You're making no sense, child. Nothing can be worse than this.'

Another bomb boomed outside; debris and dust rushed along the tunnel. Rebecca began to sob. Her words jerked out between ragged breaths. 'It's so far away. So much could go wrong. If they go, we'll never see them again.'

Her father pulled her close for another hug. 'All shall be well.'

People in the tunnel coughed and choked in the gloom; children cried with fright. The bulbs flickered on and off before settling down to light the dim space once more.

'Good job I didn't fancy Canada in the end, then,' said a voice.

Rebecca looked beyond her parents to where her sister sat on a blanket; both children cuddled against her. Snug as a bug, the three were sheltering in a curved section of the wall that was an escape hatch for Tube workers. She screamed with delight.

'Only decided this morning,' said Dot. 'As if this Blitz were something better.' She laughed. 'Those bloody Germans won't drive me abroad.'

For a moment, Rebecca felt pinned to the floor by an overwhelming sense of relief. As a grin spread across her lips, she felt a chill on her cheek, exactly like a tiny child's kiss.

Chapter Thirty-Two

The children had been right to warn her, Rebecca realised afterwards. The *City of Benares* was torpedoed five days out of Liverpool. Many lives were lost, including those of evacuee children. It put an end to the practice of sending children overseas for safety. Dot's reluctance to leave England, despite the Blitz, had saved all their lives. Their parents had argued for them to take the opportunity, but she wouldn't go without them, and there weren't enough places for the whole family.

'Besides,' Dot confessed to Rebecca later. 'I had the weirdest dream.'

'About two children?'

'How did you know that?'

'Never mind. What did you dream?'

'That I was about to get on that ship with my two. We were walking across some grass with these two strange kids. You were chasing us, shouting. Though I couldn't tell what you were telling me. Then I fell into the water. We all did, and I knew I was drowning.'

'Just like my premonition.'

Dot hugged her sister. 'Thanks for the warning, sis.'

Trevor stayed with his gran at the Spread Eagle pub for many weeks. With his persuasion, all of Rebecca's family moved to live there. Her parents lodged in and helped run the pub. Dot found a job as a cook at the local big house, Nostell Priory, and a tied cottage went with it. The children developed strong Yorkshire accents that made them almost incomprehensible to Rebecca when she visited them on leave.

Bomber Command needed both their services. The scarring on Trevor's hands left him unable to fly, and they soon found him a post teaching navigation at RAF Cranwell. Rebecca stayed in the WAAF, quickly becoming an expert in any new equipment that helped improve their work. She rose to the rank of sergeant herself. They spent all their leave time together and married in 1943.

That year, RAF Watton was handed over to the USAAF, who continued to use it throughout the war in Europe.

No one on the base ever mentioned seeing the children again. Perhaps Americans, being such practical people, don't see ghosts.

Thus wander'd these two babes,
Till death did end their grief,
In one another's arms they dy'd,
As babes wanting relief.
No burial these two pretty babes
Of any man receives,
Till Robin-red-breasts painfully
Did cover them with leaves.

Chapter Thirty-Three

Adrian was on his third coffee. One for the first half, one in the interval and one for the second half. It would help keep him awake on the drive home. He hated pantomime and always dreaded spending Christmas Eve in Norwich. The tradition of taking the family to this particular matinee had been part of his life since he was a child. It had started with his grandfather and then was carried on by his father, who brought Adrian and his sister until they were far too old to be anything but embarrassed by the whole affair. His father clearly enjoyed having the excuse to go, and Grandad accompanied them for years. So now Adrian continued the tradition in as much as he drove his mother, his wife Helen and the two girls to the Theatre Royal, then sat in the cafe bar while they enjoyed themselves in the auditorium. Nothing and no one would ever persuade him to be inside listening to the damn thing.

'Not your kind of show?' asked the waitress who brought the coffee jug to offer him a refill. He nodded, and she poured the stewed coffee left over from the interval into his cup.

'No, not my thing at all,' he said. 'I prefer football.'

No doubt she had him down as a philistine, Adrian thought as the woman returned to the bar and began to tidy up. He was the only person sitting in the first-floor café, scrolling aimlessly on his mobile, checking his social media. A wave of 'Oh yes it is!' burst out through the doors as an audience member escaped to the toilet. He shuddered. He wanted a pint, but it wouldn't do for him to be stopped and breathalysed. Traffic would love to pin one on CID.

More time passed, during which he purchased and consumed a rather large slice of Victoria sponge from the waitress.

'You got far to drive?' she asked as she handed him a fork wrapped in a paper napkin.

'Watton. Why?'

'The snow.'

Watching the large, soft flakes falling on the terrace beyond the glass doors made him feel even grumpier. It was settling on the outside tables and chairs. Hopefully, the roads might be a different matter. Surely the council would be keeping them clear.

Guessing from the level of applause that the show was ending, Adrian drank his last mouthful of cold coffee and went downstairs to wait for his family. The quiet of the nearly empty foyer emphasised the grey-white skies outside. Even the box office was closed; most of the city's workers would have long since gone home. The auditorium doors opened, releasing the excited audience, who streamed out, carried on a tidal wave of Christmas spirit.

'It was marvellous,' Helen assured him as he guided them out onto the street through the milling crowds of shouting children. 'So brave of them to do *Babes in the Wood*.'

'Brave?'

'It's supposed to be unlucky, you know?'

'No, I didn't know. Why's that?'

'With it being a local story. Your mother was telling me.'

'We're all going to be unlucky if we don't get a move on,' said Adrian. The snow was settling on the pavement. His daughters squealed with delight.

'Oh! A white Christmas. How perfect,' said his mother.

'Only if we get home before we have to dig out the drive.'

By the time they had found the car in the nearly deserted underground car park and manoeuvred their way out of the place, the snow was falling hard. It was settling on the roads and buildings. His mother sat in the back seat, between the girls. For a few minutes, they sang the *Ghostbusters* song, with the hand actions the Pantomime Dame had taught them. Slowly the purr of the car quieted them, and the children's eyes began to droop. Adrian drove in concentrated silence until they crossed the bypass, then curiosity got the better of him. After all, he was a detective inspector.

'Why is it an unlucky play, Mum?'

'It's only unlucky in Norfolk, I think. You know the story, don't you?'

'Two small children, left to starve in the woods by their wicked uncle.'

'Nursey helps to save them,' said his elder girl with a yawn. 'And Robin Hood.'

'Robin Hood?'

'I don't think he was in the original story.' Helen smiled.

'They added that when it became a panto. It says so in the programme.'

'So why is it special here?'

'The woods in question are supposed to be Wayland Woods.'

'Our Wayland Woods?' Adrian was surprised. 'I never knew that.'

'Really, darling!' Helen laughed. 'You don't pay much attention, do you, for a detective. It was the first thing everyone was keen to tell me when we moved to Griston.'

Adrian grunted because he knew she had a point. Much of his job depended on analysing people, the things they said or their body language. Away from work, he tried to switch off all that observation and tended to leave the socialising to his wife. If Adrian thought about his neighbours very much, he might end up being suspicious about everything. He could always spot when something wasn't right, when it was out of character or in the wrong place. His boss told him that was why he was a good copper. Helen got to know most people in the area, as she worked three mornings a week as a receptionist at the local doctor's surgery.

'Anyway,' said his mother. 'It's that wood, the one we pass when we turn off the Norwich Road. But it's only a story, I suppose.'

Chapter Thirty-Four

It wasn't only the children who had drifted off to sleep as Adrian turned the car off the main road. His mother was dozing with her chin on her chest. The snow was falling steadily, swirling in the gusts of wind, forming shapes before becoming a blanket of uniform whiteness. It was hard to find the turning for the narrow country lane that led to Griston. There was no sense of how far they had travelled or how long they had been driving. This road must be a low priority for the council, as it hadn't been cleared. Helen was staring at the snow, which was sweeping across the windscreen ferociously. She was hanging onto the door handle, Adrian noticed. He knew she was frightened.

'Not far now,' he said. He was trying to reassure her, even though he also felt worried. There was no way to identify the edge of the road. The snow covered everything, and beyond the circle of the headlights, it was pitch black. If he'd been on his own, Adrian knew he'd be going faster and taking the risk. Not with his entire family in the car.

Is this the bend in the road, he wondered, *or have I lost my bearings entirely?* He clenched his teeth in concentration.

Turning the steering wheel made the car begin to dance on the snow. The back wheels twitched left and right. It took all of Adrian's advanced police driving training to keep them from spinning. As he was beginning to regain control, his heart leapt into his mouth. Through the driving snowflakes, Adrian saw that he was about to hit two small children. They stood holding hands in the middle of the road. Their eyes were wide, like frightened animals, and they were staring straight at him. Adrian stamped on the brakes, and the car skidded violently.

Helen shrieked as the car spun in a full circle, gaining in velocity as the tyres failed to find any grip. As Adrian struggled to regain control, the vehicle switched right and crashed down a ditch at the side of the road. For one terrible moment, he thought it would turn over on its roof, but it came to rest the right way up. The nose was deep in the ditch, the back of the car off the ground. He glanced across at his wife, who was already undoing her seatbelt.

'You all right?'

'Think so,' she said and pushed at the passenger door.

In the back seat, their daughters were crying with fright as he clambered out of the car and scrambled up the bank.

'What are you doing?' Adrian shouted to the two children. 'Do you need any help?'

The skid had only carried them a few yards, and the children stood on the edge of visibility. Still shaking with adrenaline, he took a few steps towards them. 'Who's with you? What's going on?'

Helen had opened the rear door to unpack their younger

daughter. His mother pulled anxiously at her seatbelt, groaning as it released.

'Where are you?' his wife called angrily. No doubt she was as shocked as Adrian was.

He strode back to help her. 'I'm sorry. I had to avoid those kids.'

'What kids? There's no one there.' Helen peered into the snowy lane.

Adrian looked again. She was right. The lane was empty. At least it was as far as he could see, which wasn't all that far.

'Must have been the snow.'

Helen and his mother pulled out the two girls and scrambled up the bank as Adrian walked around the car to check for damage. The bonnet was crumpled, and the underside was probably wrecked, but at least the windows were intact. There was no way he would be able to reverse the thing back out. Headlights approached along the road. He was relieved to see it was a Land Rover.

'You all right?' the driver asked, pulling up beside them. 'I was checking the sheep, and I heard the bang.'

'I don't think I can get it out on my own,' said Adrian.

'Where are you heading?'

'Griston,' said Helen. She sounded tearful to Adrian.

'Oh! Hello, Mrs Hopper,' said the driver. 'Didn't see you there. Shall I give you all a lift home?'

'I should call the recovery people,' said Adrian. Helen shook her head. Her face looked white as she carried their younger daughter hitched up on her hip. The child's face was buried in her mother's neck. Adrian's mother was trembling with shock or cold, clutching her other granddaughter to her side.

'No one will come out this late on Christmas Eve,' said Helen. 'Let's just lock it up and leave it.'

'I don't suppose anyone can steal it like this,' said Adrian. 'We'd be grateful, Mr...?'

'Foster. David Foster. Jump in then.' He turned the Land Rover deftly around and got out to help them.

'How do you know Mr Foster?' Adrian asked Helen.

'Through the surgery. We look after your wife, don't we?'

'And very kind with her you are too.'

'Well, I'm very grateful for your help,' said Adrian. 'We're not taking you out of your way, are we?'

'Not at all,' said Mr Foster. 'I live at Griston Hall.'

Chapter Thirty-Five

❦

They were all rather shaken. Helen put the children to bed, their excitement from the panto and Christmas Eve subdued by the accident.

'They'll be all right,' Adrian's mother assured him. 'How about you?'

'I feel stupid,' said Adrian. 'All that special driver training, and I couldn't keep the car on the road in a little bit of snow.'

'Hardly a "little bit" if you look now.'

The snow was falling heavily, their footprints on the driveway already filled in. At least their home still had power. The heating kept the cold at bay, and the Christmas decorations made the house feel festive. As soon as Helen gave him the all-clear, Adrian piled the presents underneath the tree. Then they all headed for bed.

Adrian felt very guilty on Christmas morning. Helen had a large bruise on her forehead, presumably as a result of the accident. It made her look as if he had hit her. The girls ran downstairs and enthusiastically handed out presents before ripping the paper from their own. The rest of the morning continued as if nothing had happened yesterday. His mother and Helen were busy in the kitchen. He encouraged the girls to dress warmly and took them outside to build a snowman. Giggling and sliding, the three rolled giant snowballs, which Adrian stacked. The girls decorated the face with a traditional carrot, twigs and pebbles for the eyes. He hadn't had this much fun with them in ages.

Christmas dinner was served on the dot at one o'clock, followed by the obligatory flaming pudding, which only Adrian's mother liked and ate. Helen brought out a glorious trifle for the rest of them. Stuffed and sleepy, the family settled down to watch the afternoon child-friendly film. Before long, he drifted off to sleep, a daughter snuggled in each arm. Waking with a start just before the Queen's speech, Adrian stretched and stood up.

'I think I ought to go and check on the car before it gets too dark,' he said.

'Really?'

'I'll turn back if the snow is too bad, I promise.'

Wrapping himself up, he left the rest to their film. The snow covered everything, and the village was sparkling. It took him a while to trudge past the other houses and onto the lane. A few cars had made the journey during the day, and Adrian could walk in the tracks they had left. He reckoned it was no more than a mile to where they had come off the Watton road.

'Damn it,' he said. 'I nearly got them home. Too much caffeine, not enough sleep.' Stupid bugger.

Traffic was usually light on Christmas Day, but when he reached the junction, Adrian saw that there had been enough cars on the larger road to begin to clear it. The resulting slush was sprayed onto the verges. In the cold of the afternoon, it was starting to freeze. The tarmac was clear, if wet, and he made good time reaching the car as the light began to fade.

'Shouldn't have had a nap,' Adrian said to himself. 'It's going to be dark by the time I get home.'

The car was where they had abandoned it. The damage to the bonnet was covered by a layer of snow, which he swept off with his gloved hands. There was definitely no way he was going to be able to drive it. Once he got home, he would call his recovery service and arrange for it to be towed away tomorrow. Some poor soul might be at the call centre, but he didn't want to call out anyone on Christmas Day. The vehicle was stable, so he opened the doors and took out the girls' travel toys. He couldn't leave their favourite things behind. Stuffing them into his coat pockets, Adrian locked up and scrambled back to the road.

The snow had begun to fall again. The growing dusk was making visibility poor. Adrian knew he would need to be careful walking back, and keep listening for any approaching vehicles. Switching on the torch app on his phone, he checked down the road for traffic and zipped his jacket tighter. For a moment, the torchlight fell on the field hedge, and he thought he saw movement. Taking a few steps towards it, he suddenly saw two small faces peering at him. It was those damn children again.

Adrian didn't believe in ghosts. He had no truck with his mother's view that they were lost souls looking for rest. He did believe that children should be protected.

'You two,' he called. 'Don't go. I'll help you.'

He scrambled back down into the ditch and struggled through the snow in the bottom before pulling himself up by the dead grass on the other side.

'Why are you out here?' Adrian called loudly. 'Is anyone with you?'

There was a small gap in the hedge. If this was Mr Foster's land, then he kept it neat for the most part. Adrian struggled to push through into the ploughed field beyond. The children were standing several yards away from him. They were waiting, staring at him, hand in hand. He gestured to them.

'It's all right. I'm a police officer. I won't harm you. I'll get you home.'

The boy gestured at Adrian as if beckoning to him. Then the pair turned their back on him and walked away across the field. Adrian began to stumble after them, feeling angry and perplexed. The ploughed earth under the snow made it difficult to walk. The ground undulated. The mud under its white cover was heavy and soon caked his boots and trousers. It didn't slow down the children, who kept a constant distance ahead of him, which made him even more frustrated. He was trying to help them, for goodness sake.

The snow was turning into a blizzard. The wind whipped the flakes, and they battered his face. He could hardly see his feet, let alone where he was going. But somehow, the children walked ahead of him at the edge of his vision. Adrian struggled on until the field ended abruptly in a wire fence with a wood beyond. He climbed through, following the children, who seemed untroubled by the wind and dizzy dancing snow.

Under the trees, the snow was massing into small drifts

before being whirled up again. Adrian laboured on, the clinging mud slowing him down, even under the trees. There was little light here. What there was reflected off the snow and outlined the obstacles. He shone his mobile torch around, picking out what seemed to be a path. The children were waiting there. Adrian followed them deep into the wood until, exhausted, he leant one hand against a massive tree trunk and struggled to catch his breath. His body was warm from exertion, but his face was painfully cold. The feeling in his fingers had vanished, despite his thermal gloves. Sweat trickled down his back; his arms and legs ached with the effort.

As his heart calmed, he looked around to try and get his bearings. The children stood motionless, watching him, waiting. Calmness drifted over him. His body urged him to sit down and wait out the storm.

Maybe this is the beginnings of hypothermia, he thought. *I should keep moving.*

Adrian was confused as he looked at the children again. They were young. The boy was taller than the girl. Neither could be more than five or six years old. The girl clung to the boy's hand as though her life depended on it. Which indeed it did on a night like this in the middle of nowhere.

It isn't nowhere, Adrian realised. *We're in the middle of Wayland Woods.*

'Where are you taking me?' he called. The snow-laden trees muffled his voice.

The boy beckoned. With a huge effort, Adrian pushed himself away from the tree and ploughed on. They left the path and walked into the densest of the woodland. The canopy of the trees let in little snow, and it grew harder to see. Dead brambles and bracken impeded Adrian, pulling him back one step for every four that he took.

Now the boy was pointing to the ground, where it rose into a mound. Adrian shone his torch at the spot. Under a light sprinkling of snow, there appeared to be a badger sett. He might be a town boy, but Adrian had been with the Norfolk Police long enough to have taken part in jobs that tried to catch those who dug up the poor creatures for baiting.

'Is this it?' he asked. 'You've dragged me here because you're upset by someone trying to trap badgers?'

Struggling closer, Adrian inspected the sett. There were two deep holes, several feet apart. The remains of a fresh scrape or spoil heap lay in front of one of them.

'Glad they're keeping warm,' Adrian muttered, wishing he could do the same.

When he looked up, the children had gone. As though they'd only been illusions of the snow in the wind and had blown away in the night.

Feeling bewildered, Adrian shone his torch in an arc and tried to call to the children. His voice was dampened by the snow. Sweat was beginning to dry on his back under his coat. Pulling his daughter's bunny comfort blanket from his pocket, he tied it as firmly as he could to a sturdy-looking branch as a marker. He knew he needed to get back to the road, and then he would be able to get home. Stamping his feet to warm them, he wondered if the night could get any worse. And then, of course, it did.

The ground under his feet gave way, pitching Adrian heavily onto his knees. Cursing, he could feel himself sinking into a pit. He was already knee-deep and put out his hands to save himself. As he leant on the ground, another section collapsed. His mobile flew from his grasp. The torch flicked off. In the snow bright night, a dark patch of earth opened up with a pale grey patch in the centre.

It's just a root, Adrian assured himself as he put his hand on it, *a dead animal maybe*.

It was small and dead, sure enough. But it was no animal. Adrian had been a copper for more than twenty years and a detective for twelve of those. He'd seen some things in that time. Leaning back against the mound of collapsed earth with a sigh, Adrian knew that he was looking at a human skull. A small one. It could only belong to a child.

Chapter Thirty-Six

❦

Helen and his mother were frantic by the time Adrian reached home. He'd been missing for hours. He'd lost his mobile in the dark near the badger sett. The sight of his muddy, soaking figure walking tiredly past the snowman in the garden had brought them outside shouting and crying. Too exhausted to explain, he had allowed them to cosset him with a warming soak in the bath and a luxury hot chocolate. Lying there in the water, Adrian tried to work out what he should do about his find. If, indeed, it was a find and not a hallucination. At any event, there was nothing he could do tonight.

On Boxing Day, his breakdown service managed to find a local garage that would come and tow the car out of the ditch. The storm had passed and the roads were clearing, though the snow was still deep on the fields and verges. Helen took him in her car to meet the tow truck. As they watched the truck winching Adrian's car, Mr Foster pulled up in his Land Rover.

'How is it?' he asked.

Adrian grimaced. 'We'll see when they get it inside. Not good, though, I suspect.'

'Are you all well?'

'Yes, thanks,' said Helen. She shivered with cold. 'I'm going to sit in my car for a bit, put the heater on.'

Mr Foster stood next to Adrian, interested in the proceedings. 'Thought I saw you yesterday, about tea time? Walking on the road?'

'Yes, that was me. I came to make sure it was still here.'

'Didn't see you go back.'

'No.' Adrian shivered.

'You should get in the car if you're cold.'

'I'm not cold. I think I might be unwell, though.' He tried to smile, but it didn't come off.

'Oh?'

'Must be going down with something. Because I keep seeing things.'

'What sort of things?' Mr Foster sounded cautious.

'Not things, actually. Two young children.'

'Along this road?'

Adrian turned to look at the farmer. 'Yes, just here. I thought I saw them in the headlights. That's what made me brake and end up down there.'

'Like the babes in the wood?'

'To be fair, I put it down to the fact that we'd just been to see that exact pantomime in Norwich. Like it was playing on my mind.'

'Now you don't think so?'

'Yesterday, when I came to check on the car, I saw them again.'

'The boy is taller than the girl?'

'Yes! How do you know?'

Mr Foster pointed over the hedge. 'My farm is the old hall that was the cause of the crime.'

'The one they were supposedly murdered for?'

'That's right.'

'How did this story come about?'

'There were rumours at the time. Then a chap called Thomas Millington from Norwich published what they call a broadside ballad about it. After that, it passed into folklore.'

'When was this?'

'Elizabethan times. I see them myself sometimes in the field there. I tried to follow them once. But I couldn't catch up with them. I had the sheep in this field then, and it was nearly lambing. Thought I was just overtired.'

'I tried to catch them too.'

'No good?'

'No. Followed them into the woods.'

'In that storm? Madness.'

'I know.' Adrian shuddered. 'I thought I was going to die of exposure.'

'Lucky you didn't. Seeing the children is supposed to be a warning. Over time, people said it was unlucky to see them.' Mr Foster laughed. 'I'm a bit of a buff for local history, you know.'

'What sort of warning?'

'Sometimes it's personal, like a death in the family.'

'And other times?'

'Some sort of national tragedy or emergency, like the war, or a disease like the smallpox epidemic that killed half the children in Griston. That was back in Victorian times.'

'Why now? There's no war imminent as far as I know.' Adrian frowned. 'If they are supposed to be giving a warning, why would they want me to follow them?'

Mr Foster's face wrinkled with concentration. 'Never heard of that before. Are you sure that was what they wanted?'

'They kept stopping to make sure I was still there. The boy beckoned to me. And then I found something.'

'Somewhere in the woods?'

The tow truck driver came to say he was ready to leave. Arranging to give the car a look on the next working day, he drove off to Thetford.

'I was on my way to take the dogs for a run in Wayland Woods,' said Mr Foster. 'They get stir crazy if there's not much to do. Why don't you tell your wife to go home and get warm? You can come with me if you like.'

There was a small car park at the entrance to the woods. They left Mr Foster's Land Rover there, released the two collies and set off down one of the better-used footpaths. The snow crunched under their boots, though there had been quite a few walkers already making tracks this morning.

'Popular spot for an outing,' said Mr Foster. The dogs sped about under the trees and along the path ahead of them. They soon left the wider track and followed the dogs along a less well-defined trail. 'Lots of circular walks here.'

The further away they walked from the car park, the less the tracks had been used. Adrian looked around. Trying to get his bearings, he pointed to a lighter area through the trees. 'Is that your land?'

'Yes.'

'I followed them across your field.' Mr Foster gave him a look of disapproval. 'At least I think it was. Sorry.'

'Never mind. Then, what?'

'They brought me in here somewhere. It was hard to see, and I wandered off the footpath into a wild area. Then they stopped.'

'And?'

'It was a badger sett.'

'You should have said.' Mr Foster sounded cheerful. 'Only one of those in here. Not many folks know about it. A few of us try to keep an eye on it, stop them baiting buggers from getting at it.'

He whistled the dogs back to him and set off with a purposeful stride. Adrian had to hurry to keep up. The farmer pushed through an area of undergrowth, knocking snow from over-laden branches and holding aside brambles with his walking stick for Adrian to get through. Eventually, he stopped and made the dogs wait by a tree. Creeping forward, with Adrian crunching clumsily in his wake, Mr Foster headed for a small clear area. There was much less snow here, the ground clearer.

The bunny comfort blanket hung, forlornly, from the branch where Adrian had tied it. Meltwater dripped from the rabbit's nose. A silver glint caught Adrian's attention. With luck, it was his mobile phone.

'That's it,' said Adrian. He stepped forward but Mr Foster grabbed his arm.

'Steady now,' he said. The place is riddled with tunnels. You have to be careful.'

'I know,' said Adrian. 'I fell into one of them. Come and see.'

The two men walked across the snow to the sett entrance.

'There, see?'

Mr Foster scanned the disturbed earth.

'It went from under me. But look there.'

'Do you mean that?' The farmer asked, pointing with his stick. The pair moved closer. Something small and ivory-coloured stood proud of the loose dark soil.

'What do you think it is?'

'Well, as you ask me, I'd say it was bones. Maybe a skull?' He moved in for a closer look.

'That's what I thought too. Please don't touch it. I think this is a crime scene.'

Chapter Thirty-Seven

※

Technically, Adrian was correct. It was a crime scene. Just a very old one.

'You need an archaeologist, not a pathologist,' said the crime scene investigator. 'Whatever is going on here happened decades ago. Centuries perhaps.'

The archaeological team came out between Christmas and New Year. Fortunately, there had been little fuss. Adrian's find didn't make the local news until later on. That meant no illegal detectorists got wind of it or pillaged the site before the emergency digging team arrived. Once they began the excavation, the story spread quickly. Adrian suspected that one of the diggers leaked information, but it didn't seem worth saying anything as no damage was done to the find.

There was limited time at the site, the days being short. Even so, the team soon identified the skeletons of two small children. The male one was larger than the female.

'Poor souls could only have been about six or seven,' the

lead archaeologist told Adrian. 'I think the badgers must have disturbed them when they were digging in the sett.'

'Anything that could identify them?'

She offered him a shallow tray with two plastic bags in it. 'You can take them out if you want.'

Adrian opened the first bag. It contained a gold ring with a red stone. Two tiny initials were engraved on the gem. He held it up to the light and looked more closely.

'Garnet, I'd say. We'll get that confirmed. The initials seem to be G and R.'

'I wonder what they stood for,' said Adrian. He weighed the ring in his hand. It felt like a feather.

'It's too big for a child, wouldn't you say? Yet it was on the finger of the female.'

'Why would she have it?'

'I can only speculate that it belonged to a parent.'

'Maybe their dying mother gave to the little girl.'

'Perhaps. Anything is possible.'

The second bag held a buckle of some sort.

'Most likely on a cloak, rather than a belt, as it was near the boy's neck.'

Adrian didn't want to think about the implications of a belt around a six-year-old boy's neck. 'Were they dumped here? Can you tell?'

'To some extent,' she said. 'The badgers may have moved the bones around. Even so, it looks as if they were sleeping. The boy had his arms around the girl like he was hugging her.'

'In your opinion, is it the babes in the wood?'

'We'll never be absolutely sure.'

'What will happen to them now?'

'Back to the archives for examination first thing. Then we'll have to see.'

Despite the archaeologist's caution, Adrian was certain. His mother agreed with him.

'It is the babes,' she said. 'I've always thought that story was true. The original one, I mean. Not the pantomime. They were left to die.'

'We may never be sure who they are,' he said. It was as if he were trying to convince himself. 'They may have been runaways or something.'

'I know it's your job to consider all the possibilities. But you know, just like I do. It's the babes from Griston Hall. Murdered by their uncle so he could inherit their money. It's always the money, isn't it?'

'Often. Not always.'

'Anyway, they belong here. Not in some box in the archive. Don't they have to rebury bodies these days?'

'It's not my area of expertise,' said Adrian. 'I can find out.'

Chapter Thirty-Eight

They reburied the children in Griston churchyard with a full and proper funeral service. Most of the village attended, as did quite a few of the press. A collection had been made for a headstone to mark the grave.

Two children, aged six and four.
Known unto God and beloved of their community.

Mr Foster attended and stood with Adrian to watch the tiny coffins being lowered into the earth. As they turned to leave, Adrian thanked him for his help.

'My pleasure,' said Mr Foster. 'Poor souls. Out there alone all these years.'

'You know about these stories. Why do you think they wanted me to find them?'

'You're still convinced they wanted that?' Adrian nodded. Mr Foster continued, 'Well, I'd say there are two possibilities. The pragmatic one is that the badgers disturbed them.'

'And the other?'

'That you reminded them of someone, like their uncle?'

'A police detective that resembles a murderer!' Adrian smiled. 'I certainly could murder some of those buggers I have to deal with. Take care, Mr Foster.'

That evening the family settled down to eat their tea and watch the news. There were pictures of the funeral on the local programme. Adrian had declined to give an interview.

'I hope the poor babes are happy,' said Adrian's mother, 'now that they have found peace.'

'Let's hope there are no more sightings,' agreed Helen. 'Then there will be no more premonitions of danger.'

They didn't pay much attention when the newsreader moved onto a story from China.

'The Chinese Government have today denied that a new and virulent form of flu is causing them problems. An outbreak similar to that of SARS in 2003 has been raging through the city of Wuhan. Now the city is to be locked down to prevent the outbreak from spreading further.'

Afterword

Some things you might like to know

Writing any story based in a historical period is fraught with potential pitfalls. Any inconsistencies in these stories should be put down to either my lack of accuracy or poetic licence. My aim is to entertain. However, you might like to know some of the following.

The Babes in the Wood – A Norfolk Folktale

The Norfolk folk tale's first known mention is an anonymous broadside ballad published by Thomas Millington in Norwich in 1595. The story appears in various collections of fairy tales and children's poems from the beginning of the nineteenth century to the present day.

Two children, a brother and sister, are left in their uncle and aunt's care after their parents' death. The young pair have also inherited a valuable hall and farm. If anything

AFTERWORD

happens to them, everything passes to their uncle. After many months, the uncle tires of looking after the children and decides to get rid of them. He hires two ruffians to take the children away and kill them while telling his wife that he is sending them to London to be educated. The ruffians take the children into the nearby woods but can't bring themselves to kill the innocent babes and abandon them to their fate instead. Unable to find their way out, the two children eventually lie down under a tree. Birds cover them with leaves, where, despite this kindness, the two die of cold and hunger.

The folk tale appears to have been based on the true family tragedy of the de Grey family. They owned Griston Hall between 1541 and 1572. In this case, young Thomas de Grey was due to inherit the hall when his grandfather died. Being a child, he was left in the care of his uncle, Robert de Grey, and his stepmother. All seemed well until his stepmother remarried four years later, moving away to Baconsthorpe. Eleven-year-old Thomas set out on a journey to visit her but never returned. When his uncle, Robert, claimed the hall as his inheritance, rumours flew.

The town of Watton and the village of Griston have long claimed the story as their own. Wayland Woods, which lies between the two, are reputed to be the site where the children were abandoned. It is a public space where visitors can walk at leisure. Their ghosts are regularly reported as being seen, and the woods are known locally as the Wailing Woods as a consequence. To see the children is considered a dire warning of either personal or national calamity.

AFTERWORD

Pantomine

British theatres have a long history of pantomime, although the type of show the word describes has changed over time.

Early pantomimes were comic interludes, originally based on Italian commedia dell'arte characters. There was little or no dialogue (hence 'mime'), and they could be seen as part of an evening's entertainment in theatres, music halls and animal shows, such as Astley's Equestrian Circus. These performers are best thought of as being similar to the clowns in modern circus troupes. These interludes were also called harlequinades.

By the mid-Victorian period, pantomimes had begun to morph into full-length family entertainments based on well-known fairy tales. They usually starred the most famous music hall entertainers of the day, such as Dan Leno and Marie Lloyd. By the beginning of the twentieth century, these shows were firmly part of the British Christmas season. The traditions of cross-dressing, particularly the Dame being played by male comics and the principal boy being played by a pretty young girl, were all established during this time.

The first known version of *The Babes in the Wood* as a pantomime is believed to date from 1827. By the 1860s, Robin Hood and Maid Marian's characters had been added to give the story the happy ending that we would recognise today. Dan Leno appeared in a sumptuous version at Drury Lane in 1897.

Today the story would usually include a Wicked Baron (or uncle); two inept robbers/murderers (often played by a known double-act); the children's nurse (the Dame); the Merry Men, with Robin and Marian; a principal boy and girl

AFTERWORD

and, of course, the two children. It remains a firm favourite and is regularly produced around the UK at Christmas, though rarely in Norwich.

Broadside Ballads

Ballads have a long history, reaching back to Medieval times. Minstrels would learn lengthy songs with a regular structure and rhythm. Travelling around the country, they would sing them wherever they stopped. It was an easy way to remember and repeat news or stories, allowing them to be spread amongst populations where reading was a rare skill.

Broadside ballads became popular after the advent of printing in the sixteenth century. Small presses were set up in most centres of trade and/or learning and printed these song sheets in large quantities. Printed on a single side of a large sheet of paper, the ballads were easy to produce and cheap to buy. They often recounted local stories or folklore, and many people learned to read because of the songs' widespread distribution. Written music was not readily understood or fully formalised in Tudor times, so the verses would be adapted to a tune that local people already knew.

Little is known about Thomas Millington of Norwich, except for this ballad. It doesn't seem unfair to assume he was one of those small printers whose workshops sprang up during Elizabeth's reign. The ballad itself was reprinted many times over the centuries, and copies from the 1650s onwards survive in various library archives. The verses quoted in the story are from the Millington ballad, and the full song is available online as a facsimile or as lyrics.

AFTERWORD

History – sort of

I have long been a history lover, studying it as part of my degree with the Open University. So, the stories written here have some basis in fact. Which bits are fact and which are fiction, I leave up to you.

1649

Many wonderful books can be found about the English Civil War if you would like full information. Like all historical periods, it is subject to revision and renegotiation amongst professional historians.

In 1642 King Charles the First raised his standard at Nottingham, and war broke out between the royalist and parliamentary factions. Oliver Cromwell ultimately became the leader of the parliamentarians. Between 1642 and 1649, many battles were fought, with victories for both sides. King Charles was arrested and tried in 1649 and executed on the 30th of January. The country became a Commonwealth until 1660, despite an attempt by the heir apparent to reclaim his throne in 1651. Oliver Cromwell refused the crown, preferring to run the country as Lord Protector until his death in 1658. His son, Richard, took over as Lord Protector, resigning from the position in 1659. Charles the Second (son to Charles the First) was invited back and took up the throne in 1660.

AFTERWORD

1841

John Sell Cotman was a professional artist and a member of the Norwich School of Painters, along with others like John Crome and Joseph Stannard. Working primarily in watercolours, Cotman's works pre-figure J.M.W. Turner and the French Impressionists' more famous work. The work of the Norwich School artists has long been undervalued by the art establishment. However, primarily thanks to J.J. Colman (of Colman's Mustard fame), many of their works were saved within Norfolk. They have been on display in Norwich's Castle Museum for many years and are well worth visiting.

1899

Women's mental and physical health was a difficult subject for Victorians. In a highly patriarchal society, mental health issues, including bereavement, were dismissed as hysteria in women. Despite their fascination with death and funerals, little was understood or accepted about the processes of grief. The 1853 Lunatic Asylum Act was supposed to prevent people from being locked up without proper consideration. Unfortunately, the system was frequently abused, and husbands had the power to admit their wives with the agreement of a supposedly independent third party. Once inside, the patient had no way of leaving unless a family member agreed to be responsible for them. One famous list of reasons for admission to an asylum included 'hysteria'; 'desertion by husband'; 'time of life'; 'women trouble' and 'novel reading'.

1940

RAF Watton was opened in 1937. It was used by a variety of squadrons of Bomber Command from 1937 to 1943. The wiping out of the two squadrons in 1940 is true. In 1943 the base was handed over to the USAAF and used by the Americans as a Strategic Air Depot and for a Reconnaissance Bomber Group. In 1945 the base was handed back to the RAF, who continued to use it in various ways into the twenty-first century, when it was closed and sold off.

My special thanks to Gordon Thorburn and his wonderfully informative book *The Squadron That Died Twice* (available on Amazon).

Thanks

Much of this book was written during the various Covid lockdowns during the winter of 2020/21. Several of my writer friends and I got together regularly on Zoom and exchanged works in progress as a way of keeping cheerful. Those dark winter lockdowns seemed the perfect time to be thinking about ancient folktales and ghosts. Several beta readers have helped in their development including Wendy Turbin, Karen Taylor, Louise Sharland, Antony Dunford and Louise Mangos. You may recognise some of these names, as all are published authors. Thank you guys for keeping me sane and working! I am grateful to Rebecca Collins and Adrian Hobart for taking a punt on an unusual project. Also to Sue Davison for her wonderful editing skills, Jayne E. Mapp for the lovely cover design and my gorgeous daughter, Gwynira Daikin, for the spooky cover artwork. Last, but by no means least, I want to thank my husband, Rhett Davies. Always the first to read what I have written and my rock on a daily basis.

About the Author

Yorkshire born, Judi has lived, worked and made theatre in Norfolk for the last forty years. She completed her MA in Creative Writing (Crime Fiction) at the University of East Anglia (UEA) in 2019.

Judi has been a horror fan since her teenage years. Spurred on by BBC television adaptations of M. R. James stories, she began to read everything from Dennis Wheatley to the Pan books of short horror stories that used to be so popular. She is also one of the few people who can claim to have actually read *Melmoth The Wanderer* and other gothic classics, including, of course, *Dracula*.

Judi is also a working actor and runs her own theatre company, Broad Horizons. Recently she narrated *Sleeping Dogs* for Wendy Turbin and is looking forward to doing more of these. Her DS Sara Hirst crime novels are published by Joffe Books.

Hobeck Books – the home of great stories

We hope you've enjoyed reading this novella by Judi Daykin. To keep up to date on Judi's writing please check her website: **https://judidaykin.co.uk**.

Please visit the Hobeck Books website for details of our other superb authors and their books, and if you would like to get in touch, we would love to hear from you.

Hobeck Books also presents a weekly podcast, the Hobcast, where founders Adrian Hobart and Rebecca Collins discuss all things book related, key issues from each week, including the ups and downs of running a creative business. Each episode includes an interview with one of the people who make Hobeck possible: the editors, the authors, the cover designers. These are the people who help Hobeck bring great stories to life. Without them, Hobeck wouldn't exist. The Hobcast can be listened to from all the usual platforms but it can also be found on the Hobeck website: **www.hobeck.net/hobcast**.

Finally, if you enjoyed this book, please also leave a review on the site you bought it from and spread the word. Reviews are hugely important to writers and they help other readers also.

Also by Judi Daykin

Under Violent Skies

Set under the brooding skies of North Norfolk, meet Detective Sergeant Sara Hirst as she searches for her lost father and finds that great beauty sometimes conceals great violence.

ALSO BY JUDI DAYKIN

DS Sara Hirst has moved from London to Norfolk Police's Serious Crimes Unit. She wants to know the truth about her father, who has connections with the area. Her mother won't tell her the real story.

A new job. A new place. Same old problems.

Sara's first call out is to a decomposing body discovered in a ditch on a local farm. How does the murder relate to a recent spate of thefts? Who wanted the victim dead?

'OMG, this was one of the **best first books I have ever read.**' Denise

'What an **astonishing** debut crime novel.' Hazel

ALSO BY JUDI DAYKIN

Into Deadly Storms

Detective Sara Hirst returns to face her toughest case yet. Dawn breaks as a dog-walker finds a dead body, half-naked and wrapped tightly in an old groundsheet. Sara is first on the scene. Who is the victim? And who will be next? Sara must take on some of Britain's most wanted criminals if she's to find out the truth.

Too many secrets.

Too much pain.

Too many leads.

This crackling, twisty thriller set within the mysterious beauty of the east coast will have you flying through the pages right till the gripping end.

ALSO BY JUDI DAYKIN

'**A gritty, gripping crime novel** that reveals the tragic reality of the county lines drug business. Highly recommended.' William Ryan, author of *The Holy Thief*

'This is a gripping police procedural that is compelling and character driven. There's heart as well as suspense.' Robin P.

Both published by Joffe Books.